Taken 1

Lolita London

Copyright © 2016 by Lolita London

All rights reserved. No part of this publication may be reproduced, distributed, or transmitted in any form or by any means, including photocopying, recording, or other electronic or mechanical methods, without the prior written permission of the publisher, except in the case of brief quotations embodied in critical reviews and certain other noncommercial uses permitted by copyright law.

CHAPTER 1

The sun was setting a bright crimson as it lowered itself over Boston. Amanda sat between her sisters with a cheeky smile on her face and a mouthful of lemon drizzle cake.

"Bertha, please don't tell me that's true," she was blushing madly.

"Aaw yeah, I tell ya he's a stallion," her sister Bertha was spilling some juicy details.

Amanda clutched her hands to her ears and shook her head in embarrassment.

"I don't think I wanna hear any more of this!" she laughed.

The three sisters had a fun and rowdyrelationship and prided themselves on being fiercely honest and open with each other. Sometimes though this could border on unconventional as the two elders taught their little Amanda about the ways of the world and of course this involved a lot of sex.

"Scarlett?" Amanda turned to her other sister. "What was your first time like?"

The redhead put her fork and plate down on the floor and smiled. As per usual each evening's sundown signalled the three girls heading out to the bench on the porch with their desserts. Scarlett though, in spite of her fiery name, was a shy girl and always the last to speak. She merely enjoyed the chance to be outside in good company.

"It was…interesting," she said but didn't elaborate.

"What does THAT mean?" Amanda cried and nudged her sister with her elbow.

"Dear Lord be patient Amanda and let me speak,"

They all giggled like a gaggle of witches.

"Ok so it went like this," she began and they all leaned in. "I was working for the family over on Maple Avenue, you know that Dutch family with the pale children and no friends? Anyway I only had to watch the children for one evening a week while the parents were away doing some quaint church business. Except it was kinda fun because one of the kids was only a year younger than I was and after a few weeks I noticed he kinda had a thing for me. He was always staring and eager to keep his younger siblings under control to make my day easier. It was kinda sweet, it really was…"

"But Scarlett! He was under your care you Devil?" Amanda was outraged.

"Believe me that boy was seventeen and I was NOT the one who was a devil," she giggled. "So yeah I was there every week and got close to him you know. We'd read the same books and often we'd put the small ones to bed and then we'd sit out in the stables most the evening just talkin'. He was real nice and always asking me questions about myself and soon we were holding hands and then we'd lean into each other as we spoke. Soon enough one evening he leaned in and kissed me and who was I to stop him? He felt so warm and gentle and that evening I was practically skipping home. I felt so grown up and sexy I couldn't wait to see him again. The next time I saw Maxi, his name was, I got him into the stables quick and pounced on him. He got excited quickly and his hands were fast and eager. He was grabbing me everywhere and I didn't like it but a stern word made him slow down." Scarlett raised her eye brows and smirked as she remembered the night vividly.

"I lay him down on the hay and just sat on him. You know I wanted to be in control of HIM not the other way round. I teased him for hours and kissed his neck and then his chest. He was writhing underneath me and I loved it. Every time he thought more was coming I'd hold off and pin his arms down. He was this close I tell ya," she showed the girls with her thumb and forefinger and they all laughed.

"So just watching him be so desperate for it really got to me, I needed him. BADLY! After some considerable effort I managed to remove my undergarments. Amanda listen to me when I say that when it comes to your first time and you know it's coming, get rid of those frilly burdens beforehand. They are just a nightmare in the heat of the moment… So I wanted it bad right? But when I actually saw his…thing I was suddenly all nervous. I'd never seen one before had I? It was bigger than I expected and I was worried it would hurt. I held it in my hand and he started to push up in between my fingers like it was the best thing he'd ever felt. And just watching his face all seized up and his hips gyrating made me make up my mind pretty quickly. I sat on him and my God it stung! A truly painful experience but the pain quickly left and all I felt was……urgh just bliss girls, just bliss. It didn't last that long for either of us I tell ya," and Scarlett smiled coyly while the other two were entrenched in her story.

Amanda was barely sitting in her seat as she constantly kept moving closer to hear more.

"So when he….you know finishes. Can you feel it inside of you?"

Scarlett shook her head.

"That's kinda weird…"

"Not really." Scarlett shrugged.

"So it hurt? Does it hurt for everyone?" Amanda looked to her other sister.

"Oh yeah! It hurts for everyone and it can bleed a little too," Bertha said outright.

"Hmmmm…." Amanda toyed with a thought in her mind but before she could say anything the front door opened.

"Girls." Their mother sang. "It's time you three came inside for some hot cocoa. Don't want you catching a chill,"

And the sisters ventured inside happily to sit by the fire. Yet as the usual family evening descended into merriment and singing Amanda excused herself and sat alone in her bedroom. Still the idea of pain titillated her mind but she wasn't sure why. She lay under the covers of her luxurious bed and thought about what her sisters had said. *I don't think I'd be too worried if it hurt*, she thought to herself as her face grew pink.

Amanda always looked like a princess in her bed and felt like one too. As her luscious dark curls draped down from the pillows and framed a perfect doll like face she often lay awake at night fantasizing. Her favourite dream was that she lay in waiting like Sleeping Beauty and a handsome, strong stranger would break in through the window. She'd pretend to be asleep as he climbed in and saw her. As he'd pull back her bed sheets she'd mimic rolling over sleepily as her nightgown fell open. She knew it was a silly fantasy but something about the danger of it excited her.

She thought back to Scarlett and Maxi and how she loved being in control of him but the more she relived the story in her mind she thought that she'd prefer it to be the other way round. She imagined being pushed down into the hay with her arms pinned behind her. And the feeling of being held down as he pulled up her dress. She bit her lip and closed her eyes, if only she could find a man to be in control of her she'd be a happy lady. She lifted the covers up over her head as she moved her hand south.

CHAPTER 2

The smell of maple syrup, bacon and eggs wafted up the stairs and under Amanda's door. She loved breakfast and always eagerly went downstairs and tucked in before anyone else and this morning was no different. She dressed quickly and sauntered downstairs with a smile on her face.

"You look happy this morning," said her mother with her usual smile. "You look positively glowing in fact. I surmise that you had pleasant dreams,"

"Oh yes..." Amanda smiled feeling a little embarrassed. "Just the usual puppies and kittens," she lied albeit very obviously.

"Well dig in," he mother pushed an enormous, heaped plate of food in front of her.

"Keep eating like that and one day you'll explode," joked her father who was walking down the hallway with the morning paper.

"Oh you leave her alone Freddy, she's a growing woman," her mother stuck up for her.

"That's very true, soon enough you'll be as strong as your mom here," the old man smacked his wife's bottom with the paper.

Amanda always loved the banter and joy between her parents. After thirty years of marriage they were still like teenagers and she'd often catch them looking at each other admiringly. But growing up to be as strong as her mom? She wasn't sure about that, she wanted to be tiny and frail, a little toy that someone could play with.

"You're drifting off into a day dream," laughed her mother. "And anyway a letter came for you this morning.

She placed an ominous looking brown envelope down in front of her daughter. Amanda looked perplexed because she'd never had a letter before. Could it be from a secret admirer? Probably not.... She worried about its contents as she flicked open the envelope with a steak knife. Her nerves quickly turned to excitement as she saw the scrawling handwriting with their wonderful words of acceptance.

"AAAH! I got the job!" she screamed almost knocking over her breakfast in excitement.

Her mother flung an arm around her and smiled but the young girl was certain she saw tears in her eyes. A sadness mixed withjoy floated around the table as her father was next to congratulate her.

~

That morning a great hubbub swirled around the house as Amanda packed and said her goodbyes. She'd never been so happy to be an adult but as she looked at her sisters she felt a terrible sadness to be leaving them.

"You're leaving us behind," said Bertha as she slumped on the end of Amanda's bed. "My little baby sister is leaving us…" she wiped a tear from her eyes with the end of her dress.

"Please tell us you'll come back, we'll see you again won't we?" Scarlett was less subtle with her tears and great big globs dripped freely from her face.

"Girl, girls seriously calm down. You're acting like I'm leaving to go to my own funeral," Amanda laughed. "I'll be back at the holidays and I'll visit whenever I can,"

The girls all embraced in a big emotional circle.

"But right now I have to get my things together. I'm getting the first train in the morning," now Amanda was crying too and her tears dripped onto her hard leather suitcase.

~

The sadness in the house on the morning of Amanda's departure was the worst the family had felt. But because she was the youngest they all tried to tell themselves that she was growing up, becoming an adult. Her mother especially tried to focus on the idea that she was moving onto better things and she imagined her returning home one day with a wealthy husband and a family of her own. She gripped onto this thought as she kissed her daughter goodbye.

"I'll write every week," Amanda cried as she stepped aboard the train with a wave of her handkerchief. "And you're always welcome to visit!"

The horn sounded on the train and it was time to go. She found her compartment quickly and bundled her suitcases onto the shelves above her head. As the train moved she stuck her hands to the window like a puppy in a pet shop and passed her family for the last time. Their faces became a tearful blur as the train sped away and at last Amanda was alone with her thoughts.

Her new life as a governess was going to be a novel and exciting one. She hoped the family she'd be living with were kind and that the children were well behaved. She wondered what the home would be like and prayed that she'd have her own room. Momentarily she panicked and was terrified at the thought that it could be dangerous. Maybe they'd keep her in a cage and make her live off bird seed. Maybe they'd force her to live in a damp basement with nothing but bread and water to survive. But that was just her imagination, a powerful source of both inspiration and misery she often ran away with.

The train passed through endless fields and tiny towns and each new scene that passed by the window was a brand new experience. Amanda had rarely left Boston and had never done so alone. The butterflies in her stomach got stronger and stronger the further she left her hometown. The further west she travelled the more sparse and agricultural the landscape became. It intimidated her, the lack of tall buildings and the scarcity of the people.

After many hours Amanda grew tired and she looked out the moving window as the sun began to set. She couldn't believe that only twenty four hours ago she was idly sitting on the porch gossiping with her sisters and learning about the world. But now she was living it! Her new job as a governess was taking her to Wyoming and for all she knew it was so far away it could be like a different country. She felt that flipping feeling in her stomach again and so lay down and dreamt of the future.

~

When the young lady woke it was because a noise was heard coming up the train carriage. The conductor knocked on all the doors and shouted with an exhausted, raspy voice through his moustache.

"Wattsville, Wyoming! Comin' up!" he knocked on her door next and she sat bolt upright as though rudely awoken from a dream.

This was HER stop. She quickly gathered her suitcases and slid open the door of her compartment. She stuck her head outside the window as it slowed down and felt the fresh, unpolluted air of the countryside. This was now home.

The train came to a halt and all Amanda could hear were whistles and horns over the top of bustling people amidst their travels. Steam drifted across the station covering the faces of eager travellers. Amanda's eyes squinted as she scanned the crowd in front of her. Sat tucked away in the back corner of the platform stood an old, stoic looking lady dressed in black. A sign sat between her two outstretched hands and the words read: "AMANDA CARTER".

CHAPTER 3

The young girl was settling into rural Wyoming life well and enjoyed the space and equanimity that coated the landscape. There was one problem though and that was the children in her care. They were little Devils with the personalities of dragons whenever their parents left the house but had the temperament of angels upon their return. Amanda loathed her job and the children equally and longed for an escape from the family.

She wondered if her parents would think of her as a failure if she were to return home after only a few months. She worried dreadfully as she began to craft a letter home.

"Dear Mama and Papa

Life here is quaint and gentle but I must inform you that I feel no affinity for this family that I have been matched with. If I were to return to Boston I pray that it be possible that you forgive my futile and fickle behaviour and welcome me with open arms."

She placed her pen down on her bureau and crumpled up the letter and threw it into a corner of her room where many other scrunched up letters lay. There was no use, she'd have to stick it out and make things work. She left home as a grown woman and she wasn't returning as a little girl, with her tail between her legs. Leaning back in her chair she huffed and nibbled at her nails, a habit she had indulged herself in after leaving home.

A crunching of gravel broke her from her thoughts and she glanced out the window to see the paper boy. He was a small and sickly fellow with a mop of brown, greasy hair yet Amanda liked his tiny stature and weak voice, she found it endearing and rather sweet. Taking the steps downstairs two at a time she skipped up to the front door and went out to greet him.

"Hi David,"

"Why hello there Miss," the boy took off his hat and bowed jokingly as if in the presence of a queen.

"Are you bringing me good news today?" she asked in jest.

"Afraid not missy, just the morning paper," he handed over the local news. "Say, are you home alone today?"

"Urgh...thankfully but don't tell anybody I said so," she laughed. "The Pendles are at a family affair and a city girl like me was not to be invited," she laughed again but this time with a hint of anger in her voice.

"Well I say that's just dreadful! A lady as beautiful as you should be taken everywhere and shown off to the world," the boy said genuinely. "Why I'd take you around the world if I could."

Amanda smiled weakly and ruffled the hair on his head as she imagined she would if she had a little brother.

"Well you have a good day now young lady," and he blew her a kiss before heading up the long dirt track.

Amanda wasted no time in finding the back pages. She practically tore the newspaper to shreds and threw the unwanted pages to the ground before running back up to her bedroom. Perusing the adverts she picked up her trusted fountain pen and began to hover her hand over the paper ready to pounce when the right job popped up before her eyes. But it didn't take long:

GOVERNESS WANTED TO CARE FOR SMALL, INFANT CHILD IN SINGLE PARENT HOME. OWN BEDROOM PROVIDED. LOTS OF SPACE ON PROPERTY. PAY NEGOTIABLE. IMMEDIATE START.

Just below in miniscule writing sat an address and Amanda was familiar with the area. In fact she could walk there! She made quick plans in her mind and prayed that her current employers wouldn't return early and catch her in a state of escape. For the second time in a year she placed all her belongings into her suitcases and said goodbye to her bedroom. Except this time not a single tear fell from her face as she closed the front door behind her.

CHAPTER 4

"Haha! So you've met the Pendles then?" a strong hearty, country laugh came from the muscular man.

"I did sir, they were lovely it's just that….." Amanda couldn't make up a convincing lie.

"Weirdos? Fruitcakes? Yuh, those kids are terrible alright," that laugh came again and it warmed Amanda's heart.

Sheriff Terrence Evans was standing in his living room with a whiskey in his hand and a friendly twinkle in his eyes.

"So I gather you've made yourself acquainted with Wattsville then? It's a funny old place isn't it?" he asked Amanda and waved his glass at her. "Are you sure I can't get you a scotch and soda?"

The young girl shook her head politely.

"No thank you sir, I'm not much of a drinker," she smiled coyly.

"Well one thing you'll learn now you're away from those Pendles is that anyone in this town that's fun to be with is a drinker," and he drained his glass.

Message received, Amanda thought to herself, apprehensively.

"So you seem like a nice girl," he continued. "But I guess the real test is whether my daughter likes you. Would you like to meet her now?"

"Oh yes, I'd love to!"

As the governess walked through the house with the sheriff she couldn't help but notice the harsh wooden textures and stark personality of the place. It looked like it had been a long time since a woman had lived here but as they walked out to the back garden the tiny giggles of a princess illuminated the house. The little girl was playing in the grass and pulling flowers out of the ground with her tiny fingers.

"Helen," the Sheriff approachedthe girl so apprehensively as if she might break if he were to startle her. "I have a visitor here to see you," he pointed to Amanda and the little girl shrunk back, withdrawing into herself. "Do you think you'd like to say hello?" he asked so fearfully.

The little girl looked up to the governess with the palest blue eyes that hid a deep soul. They were rimmed by purple circles, tired and withdrawn. Platinum blonde curls cascaded down the little girl's back like a golden waterfall that accentuated the ethereal paleness of her elfin face. She was like a cherub, a little doll to be cared for unconditionally. Amanda felt the strongest compulsion to scoop her up in her arms and kiss her cheek. But as she looked at the girl's tiny, frail limbs and infantile expression she was worried she'd shatter like crystal. Amanda looked down to the sheriff who was kneeling next to the person that obviously his entire universe rotated around.

"She's the most beautiful little girl, so precious," the words didn't seem enough to describe how truly beautiful Helen was but it was all Amanda could think of. She looked into those enormous blue eyes.

"Isn't she a doll?" the sheriff replied.

Amanda knelt down beside the two of them and smiled at the little girl. She held onto one of her tiny hands and felt that they were soft like a baby's and so small that she worried they'd crumble beneath her fingers.

"Helen? My name is Amanda," she spoke so softly it was almost a whisper. "I came here because I'd very much like to look after you when your Daddy is at work. Do you think you'd like that?"

The little girl looked at the governess with suspicion in her eyes before her face softened and she nodded. It was such a slight nod that Amanda almost missed it.

"You would like Amanda to live here?" her father asked.

Again the girl nodded so slightly as if she wanted to say yes but was still unconvinced.

"You know," Amanda bowed her head, "I've looked after many little girls but never a real life princess like you,"

Little Helen was quickly won over and smiled so widely it made the two adults beam. The sheriff sat back with a sigh of relief and ran his fingers through his hair.

"Yeah you are a real princess ain't yah? And now you have your very own lady in waiting," he kissed her on the forehead. "Now if you don't mind I see that you have some official princess business to be getting on with," he pointed to a discarded flower on the ground. "So if you don't mind us, Amanda and I have to arrange official royal business inside."

The little girl nodded and then curtsied before sitting back in the grass.

"Oh my, she is just a real treasure," Amanda said as they entered the house.

"Isn't she? Looks so much like her mother," he didn't elaborate any further and Amanda was scared to ask. "Say you really got her there with that princess stuff," he chuckled.

"Oh… Don't all little girls want to be adored like royalty?"

"Well I'm not sure about that," he tucked his thumbs into his holster and rocked back on his heels. "But I can tell you that little Helen over there is the prettiest, most sweetest little girl. Real sugar plum fairy she is," and he smiled as he lovingly gazed out at her.

Amanda had never seen a man that cared so much about his child and her heart melted as she looked into his eyes. She felt a stirring somewhere deep inside of her body but quickly quashed it.

"So when would you like me to start sir?"

"Well I don't see a reason why you can't start now. Let me help you with your bags. I'll show you to your room," he led her upstairs.

Amanda was shown to a quaint little bedroom that was little more than a cupboard but would do her just fine.

"Sorry there's not much space," the sheriff said apologetically as he placed down her suitcases and saw that they filled most of the floor space.

"It's perfect," said Amanda. "Plus I have all that beautiful land outside to roam. Little Helen and I will have so much fun exploring…"

"About that," chimed in the sheriff. "She's not the most….amble child shall we say. She has certain health conditions and well she's very frail. Helen can't do the same as most children, just so much like her mother," he shook his head sadly and lit a cigarette. He blew grey smoke into the room and it shimmered in the sunlight.

"She's ill?" Amanda was confused.

"Very ill yes…I mean. She has low blood pressure, anaemia, terrible anxiety. She's prone to bouts of giddiness and over excitement. She's fainted more times than I've had hot dinners and she can become listless, picky even. I'm amazed that she likes you so much because, due to her fussiness, she's not taken to anyone else. There must be something about you," he pointed his cigarette in her direction and squinted as if he was trying to figure her out. "Well I better leave you to get unpacked. It'll be supper time for the little one soon so I'll see you downstairs when you're ready." And he stepped out to walk down the rickety wooden stairs.

As Amanda unpacked her things she heard the giggles and merry voices of the sheriff and his daughter. Looking out the window she saw them playing in the garden and her heart sang watching them. Yet something tugged at the edges of her mind. She felt like she was intruding somehow, as if she was inserting herself into the perfect family. She watched them for a long while and imagined herself, rather guiltily, as Helen's mother.

Soon enough the sheriff looked as though he had tired of playing princess and sat on the fence at the back of the house smoking and watching over his daughter. Amanda would have to admit it to herself sooner or later; he was the most handsome man she'd ever seen. The uniform especially was something she couldn't take her eyes off. The broad shoulders, the strong jaw…he was a real man alright. Her eyes moved across his police attire and fixated on the handcuffs that jangled from his hip. She felt the urge to bite her lip as she restrained some of the naughty thoughts in her head. She was here to care for a sickly child, not to fulfil a fantasy! Shoving her empty suitcases under the bed and checking herself over in the small mirror she made her way downstairs to start dinner.

CHAPTER 5

Terence strode purposely into the station and prepared himself for a busy weekend. His deputy Tony was waiting for him with an expectant look.

"So? Tell me you found the perfect person to look after my precious godchild?" the young man asked with genuine concern. He fingered his straggly beard nervously.

"As a matter of fact I have!" Terence put his feet up on his desk and sat back relaxed.

Tony, relieved, had never seen the sheriff so comfortable before. Usually at the start of every shift he'd panic about leaving Helen with the neighbours, wearing out the floors of the station with his continuous pacing.

"So who is she?"

"A wonderful Governess from Boston, a real humdinger, Helen took to her straight away,"

"That's great…but what about you?"

"What about me?"

"You like her don't you?"

"Yah well…. She's alright I guess," the sheriff said no more and just stared into space.

Tony took note of his furtive behaviour and sensed there was more than Terence was letting on.

"So I take it she's a pretty, young thing?" the young deputy prodded for more information.

"I didn't notice," Terence lit his tenth cigarette of the day.

"I can't say I believe you…" said Tony as he looked into his boss' unflinching face.

A tense silence sat between the men as they stared at the clock. Tony eventually stood up.

"I say I better go patrol the town center," he said rather unconvincingly.

The sheriff didn't respond, didn't even raise his head to acknowledge his deputy.

"You're a real closed book you know that Terrence? I bet you're a mean poker player," and Tony left the station feeling rather rejected.

Terence hadn't meant to seem so cold and he certainly didn't want to offend his closest friend. But that aloofness, that arrogance he was known for always came at a time of turmoil and had become more prevalent in recent years. He filled the room with smoke and reached into the top drawer of his desk for his not so secret bottle of scotch. He poured himself three fingers and tossed it back down his throat. He had to make those feelings go deeper down yet the more he tried the more they bubbled to the surface.

He thought of the lovely Amanda and how she had been so terrific with little Helen. Her perfect face and hourglass figure had struck him as soon as he opened the door to her. He thought now of her tiny waist and he imagined gripping it tightly with his hands, feeling his way up to her ample breasts that were barely hidden as they rose above her corset. He imagined pushing his fingers into the top of her sheer, soft blouse and pulling it back to reveal a pink and erect nipple. But then he stopped himself and sat bolt upright in his chair. The whiskey must be getting to him and making him think terrible, ungodly thoughts. There had only been one woman for Terence and she had gone long ago. That part of his life was now over.

Over the evening trouble came and went and the sheriff dealt with each person with his usual calm and no nonsense demeanour. Yet the more he tried to keep his mind on the station the more it wondered to Amanda's perfect features and lovely character. He thought that Evangeline would be disgusted with him.

He threw back another glass of scotch and looked at the clock. It was time to go home but as he went to pour himself one for the road he saw that the bottle was empty. He threw it in the trash and vowed that it would be his last. He thought back to Evangeline and thought he was doing a lousy job at keeping his promises. At least Helen was happy…for now.

~

The nights were starting to take a toll on the sheriff and he couldn't contain his yawns as he traipsed up the stairs to his front door. As he placed his hand around the door handle something made him stop dead in his tracks, voices. One was Amanda's but the other was a man's. Was she bringing men back to his home already? While she was alone with his daughter! A rage simmered beneath his skin and he stood outside the door for a moment longer to hear who it was. There was a laugh and then a giggle, a soft charming male voice serenading the young governess. His anger turned to curiosity. Who the hell was he? He placed one hand on his gun handle and pushed the door open with the other. He was ready to fight and as he entered his house like a blustering bull he was ready for guns blazing.

"Woah! You alright pal?" said the deputy's voice.

The startled Tony had practically dived behind the kitchen counters as he saw his boss enter the house with that fierce, murderous look. He'd only seen him like that twice before and he knew full well what the outcome was.

"Tony? What the hell? It's past midnight what are you doing here?"

"I'm so sorry to bother you sheriff. I didn't know what the time was," the young man looked genuinely remorseful as his big brown eyes looked up to his boss. "I was ridin' past here on my way back to the station and I wanted to check in on my god daughter seein' how you left her with a new governess n all."

"That doesn't answer my question Tony! What are you doing here past midnight?" the sheriff had calmed down but was still confused.

"Well that's kinda my fault," interrupted Amanda. "After I put Helen to bed we got talking and well…did you know this man is part Cherokee? That's so fascinating and I've never met an Indian before. We don't get many of them in Boston," she laughed lightly and her voice tinkled around the house like a wind chime as it broke the tension.

The sheriff finally removed his hand from his gun and walked out to the porch. Sitting down he rubbed his bloodshot eyes and sighed deeply. This wasn't what he wanted to be, an angry and paranoid man but for some reason he'd not been himself today. His deputy came out to be with him and sat down beside him.

"You've been drinking haven't you?" he asked worried.

The sheriff nodded and placed his head in his hands.

"It's ok pal," Tony soothed. "But I thought you left that behind?"

"Well I did… Until today."

"What changed?" but Tony knew the answer and she was standing in the kitchen behind them.

Another silence hung between them as they looked up to the stars. Tony always loved to gaze up at the universe. It calmed him and made him feel small and insignificant, at one with nature. His grandmother had often taken him out to the country and pointed out the constellations with her arthritic fingers. He missed her terribly, she'd know what to do right now. She'd always had an answer for everything.

"Don't let yesterday use up too much of today," was all Tony could say and he patted the sheriff on the back before saying his goodbyes.

CHAPTER 6

Amanda went to bed with a heavy heart. She was giddy on arrival but on her first day she'd nearly made her boss shoot his best friend. She made a mental note to not be so friendly in the future and to only keep her mind on Helen. But when she saw her boss stride into that house with his hand on his gun ready for action she had to admit that she wasn't scared, she was exhilarated. A bolt of energy had run though her as she saw that dangerous electricity in his eyes. She was hoping that after Tony left the sheriff would reprimand her in some way and she could get a glimpse of that anger again but he hadn't chased her.

In the distance she heard the heavy steps of his boots as they traipsed sleepily through the house. She longed to hear those steps stop outside her bedroom door but as they approached they calmly drifted away and down the hall to his bedroom. Amanda felt that sensation down below again but this time it was even stronger than usual. Was it because of the night's earlier drama? She wasn't quite sure. All she knew was that the more she thought of that sheriff's uniform with those handcuffs swinging at the hip the more she wanted to indulge herself.

She remembered his big sturdy hands as they held onto his cigarettes. Long fingers marked by calluses with knots of knuckles that had seen more fights than she could imagine. She wondered what they would feel like in her slender feminine hands. What the rough skin would feel like around her waist as he pushed her onto the bed. She imagined the muscular hands and strength as he gripped her neck firmly, pushing himself on top of her.

Amanda felt her undergarments grow wet and she slid her fingers beneath them. Would it be acceptable on her first night to tip toe down the hallway and into his room? To sit on the edge of his bed and demand a kiss? No, sadly not and so she entertained herself with the thought instead. Maybe one day she'd make her way down there and push open the door to see his muscular body. Shimmying over to his side she'd kiss his cheek and rock him gently awake. He'd be pleased to see her, ecstatic even and would sleepily open his eyes and pull her to his side. He wouldn't hold back and would immediately slide his hands up her nightgown, pinning her hips to the bed before climbing on top of her.

But she wouldn't be ready yet. She'd be eager to tell him she was a virgin and he'd find a thrill in being her first, an excitement that couldn't be matched. He'd savour the moment and take his time, handcuffing her to the bed and teasing every inch of her naked body. Her skin would tingle as the goose bumps rose under the touch of his lips. She'd raise her hips desperately for him and he'd lower them back down, attaching his mouth to her inner thigh and not going any further.

After hours of playing the gentleman he would eventually relent and become the beast she wanted so badly. Unable to hold on any longer he'd spread her legs apart and push himself into her, slowly at first. She'd cry a little in pain but as he'd enter her fully her body would ripple in pleasure and she'd want more.

Amanda relished the thought of him thrusting into her over and over again with her arms cuffed to the bed. Looking up she'd see his face twisted in ecstasy and sweat dripping down the center of his chest. Alone now in her bed she writhed her hips and ground her fingers into herself. She'd never wanted anyone more in her life!

Terrence had sat outside on the porch for a long while as the cool country breeze rustled over the fields in the distance. He'd made a fool of himself he was sure of that and he didn't know how he'd be able to face Amanda in the morning. But she was just a governess, why would she care what he acted like in his own house? But he knew that he did care and he'd made a terrible first impression on the young city girl that was so much more cultured and refined than he could ever be.

He crumpled his empty cigarette packet and tossed it away a little too angrily as he felt so conflicted. He wished that Amanda would leave his mind and be nothing more than an employee but he doubted that was possible. She'd stirred up some complex emotions in him that he was deeply uncomfortable with and each moment alone with her was a new challenge.

Terence walked up to bed with butterflies in his stomach and the beginnings of a hangover. As he passed Amanda's door he imagined pushing it open to find her awake and waiting for him but that guilt crept back and he kept walking up the hallway to his own bedroom. He was sure he heard the creak of her bedsprings as he walked away.

He flung himself onto his old mattress and sighed sadly. His bed was lumpy and fairly uncomfortable but it was the one he once shared with his wife and so he was reluctant to throw it away. He lay on his side still fully dressed and readied himself for another sleepless night. He looked at the portrait of Evangeline that always sat next to his pillow and longed for her so desperately. It had been three years since she died in childbirth but in Terrence's heart it may as well have been last week. Her sparkling green eyes shone from the picture so vividly and the sheriff often pretended that it was really her. He'd talk for hours to his wife about all the things their little girl was doing and he prayed that somewhere she was listening and watching over the family.

That stirring deep within him returned and he felt the unnatural compulsion to place his wife's photo face down so she couldn't be witness to his shame. He'd never felt so frustrated. Part of Terrence wanted to walk down to Amanda's room and throw her out the house to relieve himself of his problem and the other part wanted to march down there and kiss her hard.

Her startled face as he came home was still stuck in his mind. Her big pale eyes looking up at him like a fragile fawn and that whimsical and delicate laugh of hers, it was like music. His mind's eye wondered over her body and he imagined kissing the soft place on the back of her neck. She'd giggle and wriggle and lean back into him wanting more but he'd hold off, teasing her until she demanded him. He thought of lifting up her dress and gripping her thighs hard as he spread her legs apart and bent her over. He'd rub himself around her but never go inside, not until she was begging for it and then he'd thrust himself into her savagely until she screamed.

As Terence undressed for bed he pulled off his belt and wondered what it would feel like to be at the receiving end of the metal buckle and he imagined Amanda beneath it, her bottom red and sore. He wondered what the soft leather would feel like around the neck of the young governess and he cursed himself for thinking such terrible things. But as he lay on top of his bed naked he thought of nothing else as he slid his hand over his penis and imagined it was her. Her soft, feminine hands would be light and loving and her tongue would be gentle and attentive as it flicked over the tip. He longed for that feeling now and he gripped the bedsheets to stop himself running down to her immediately. He grimaced and clenched his teeth as he felt close to climax for the first time in years. Thoughts came to his mind quickly and flowed through him like a sinful river. He wanted to plough himself deep into the space between her enormous breasts and cover her chest in himself. He wanted to sit astride her and thrust himself into her mouth over and over as she sucked hungrily on him. More than anything he wanted to handcuff her to the bed and tease her infinitely. She'd writhe and scream as he pushed his fingers into her and he'd feel her pulse and clench around his fingers as she came.

He was closer now and kept the thought of her chained to his bed in his mind as he pumped his hand harder and grit his teeth tighter to stop himself from yelling. So close now, he shuddered hard, his eyes clamped shut almost as if he was pained. Almost there, his thighs shook violently and he threw his head back in ecstasy. He climaxed hard with a release that was so strong he felt for a second he had left his body. Crashing back onto the bed he panted and struggled for breath.

Terrence had never felt a release like that, an energy so strong it had taken over his entire body and mind. He had saved himself for tonight and stopped himself chasing her for now…but what about tomorrow? And the next day? He struggled to think about what would happen.

Pulling on his briefs he made his way downstairs to get a drink of water but as he descended the stairs he saw someone sitting at the kitchen table.

"You can't sleep either?" that beautiful voice again, it sang across the house.

Amanda was sitting in her nightgown with a glass of water and a rosy glow. Her eyes twinkled as she saw the sheriff in nothing but his underwear. She blushed and looked away.

"No…I mean. I don't' sleep much anyway," Terrence tried to reason but he couldn't take his eyes off the outline of her body as it shimmered through her nightgown.

"Well I better get back to bed," she sashayed away back up the stairs with a guilty look on her face.

Terrence was still breathing heavily as he turned on the tap and splashed his face with freezing water.

"Urgh…Jesus," he muttered to himself as he guzzled down water thirstily. "Just calm down Terry."

His satisfaction quickly turned to guilt as he imagined what Evangeline would have thought of his behaviour, how he lusted after a girl seventeen years younger than her and a governess too. The person who was supposed to be innocent and dependable, someone who's sole purpose was to be respectable.

He felt terrible as he made his way back upstairs but as he walked down the hallway and up to Amanda's room he saw that she'd left the door open.

CHAPTER 7

A somewhat happy yet tense and flirtatious year had passed since the arrival of Amanda. Helen had begun to enjoy her company as soon as she started and under the new governess' tender care the little girl thrived. She no longer would be found to be listless and feeling down and her laughter and hurried footsteps were now a common fixture in the house. Most importantly of all she had started to grow and fill out which showed her fondness for Amanda's cooking. Her dark rimmed eyes now sparkled with radiance and her ethereal complexion grew a pinkish glow. But to deny all her health problems would be a mistake for she still had low blood pressure and terrible anaemia that would often tire her easily and her anxiety often made it difficult for her to make friends away from home. Yet still the sheriff was eternally grateful to Amanda for her unconditional loving care.

They were both sat at the kitchen table looking out the window at Helen as she pranced in front of a parade of toys as if they were her royal subjects.

"Still the princess," Amanda smiled.

"As always," the sheriff laughed.

"Hey you like to keep her that way!" Amanda joked. "Or you wouldn't get her all those little princess dresses especially tailored for her. She's more spoiled that any child I've ever met!"

"And doesn't she deserve it?"

"Oh, well yeah! But you know….I have to say this really carefully Terry and I don't mean to offend you but…." She trailed off with embarrassment and immediately regretted what she was about to say.

Terrence looked worried. "Don't you be hiding things from me Amanda, what is it?" he spoke sternly.

"It's that…. You know spoiling Helen and treating her like royalty isn't going to bring your wife back," she blurted out and instantly felt horrible.

"You think I don't know that? She just looks so much like her I can't help it," his sadness manifested as anger and he slammed his empty mug into the sink before walking outside.

"Shit…." Amanda cursed herself before getting up to make Helen's lunch.

As the young governess set about her duties she worried about her own mother. As people always do they leave home with constant promises of regular contact that never come true. It had been months since she'd sent or received a letter from her family and she surmised that they were doing just fine without her. And that didn't bother her one bit because her mind was constantly fixed on the sheriff as she pined after him. She was certain that he liked her because she'd noticed those little sly glances and subtle movements that indicated he liked what he saw. And there was no doubt that she wanted him, she'd made it obvious. Since her first night in the house she'd left her bedroom door open to signal him being welcome but as always she'd wait for him only to hear his footsteps wonder past. She was sure though they'd hesitated many times only for him to change his mind at the last minute. Maybe tonight was the night, she told herself again.

~

Down at the station Terrence bustled into the building like a raging bull but that was nothing new. Tony tossed his boss a cigarette as he entered and greeted him like he always did.

"Sup sheriff? What's new?"

"Urgh......."

"That little governess still driving you wild?"

"As always," Terrence scrubbed his face with his hands to try and break his mind free from her.

"Why don't go for it? I can see it in both your eyes she's crazy about you too!"

"Yeah, yeah. I know, I know." Was all the sheriff could say, he knew he was passing up a chance to be with an incredible woman.

"You know boss, can I say something and you promise you won't get mad?"

Terrence nodded but had suspicion in his eyes.

"You do know that being chaste and miserable won't bring Evangeline back? She was agreat woman but I'm sorry boss, your time with her has gone and Helen deserves your happiness," Tony immediately worried about what he just said and feared a reprimand.

But his words got the sheriff thinking, that was the second time in only an hour that he was reminded about Evangeline and he knew his two closest friends were right. He sighed deeply and slumped back in his chair.

"Urgh....you're right partner. It's just that.... There's still that hope no matter how crazy and illogical it seems."

"I hear ya buddy," Tony smiled weakly and fidgeted with his keys.

Angry voices and quick steps broke the pair from their conversation and the men looked up to see a fellow officer dragging a redneck kid through the doors of the station.

"Stealing again!" shouted the officer. "This good for nothing scoundrel was caught trying to rob his grandma's house only a day after she'd taken ill."

"I'll take it from here," said the sheriff as he took the teenager from his colleague's hands.

He bundled the prisoner into one of the cells in the basement and revelled in the fact that he was alone down there and no one could hear the kid scream. As the boy's arms were cuffed behind his back he quickly lost his balance and fell on his front as he was pushed into the cell. The sheriff smirked and wondered what it would feel like to have Amanda in this position, for her to be so trapped and under his control, so immobile and so scared.

The thought disturbed him so he left him on the ground face down and locked the gate behind him.

His mind instantly went to Amanda and her delicate wrists that he'd wanted to tie down so badly. For the hundredth time he imagined her beautiful and curvy body under the control of his enormous, rough hands and he wanted to bring her down to these cells immediately. His body shook with pleasure as his hands moved quickly underneath his pants.

CHAPTER 8

"I don't think I want to play out here anymore tonight," the delicate little voice floated on the breeze.

"Why's that pumpkin? Are you getting cold?"

The little girl nodded grumpily and Amanda scooped her up in her arms and took her inside.

"Are you hungry my little kitten?" Amanda brushed her fingers through Helen's hair and placed her down at the kitchen table.

Again the little girl nodded grumpily.

"And what would you like to eat?"

"Cake…" was the reply.

"You little tinker! You can't have cake for supper!" Amanda laughed heartily. "How about some chicken? You like chicken don't you?"

That little grumpy nod again that Amanda had become so used to.

"OK! So chicken and gravy pie it is," the governess began knocking pots and pans around the kitchen.

She sensed however that the little girl sat behind her dressed as a princess was holding onto a secret. This was because every time Helen got nervous she started to chew on the frilly edges of her petticoats and said no words. Amanda kept sneaking little glances at the girl as she made dinner and thought she was definitely holding something back.

She placed the little girl's dinner down and gave her a kiss on the cheek.

"Helen? Everything ok?"

The little girl nodded as she placed a forkful of steaming food in her mouth.

"You know you can say actual words?" Amanda joked.

Again Helen just nodded but not before chewing on her dinner with a very serious look on her face.

"Please tell me kid, what's the matter?"

There was a very long pause as Helen fidgeted in her chair and played with her food, making figure of eight movements with her fork.

"I'm making the chicken swim in the gravy," was all she said.

"That's great sweetheart the chicken's going for a swim. But apart from that, you have anything to say?"

The little girl picked up her dress and nervously chewed on the lacing again. Eventually those enormous, watery blue eyes rose up to meet Amanda's and the little girl spoke:

"Are you my mommy?"

Amanda fell back in her chair with shock.

"What do you mean Helen? Of course I'm not!"

"It's just that I knew that I had another mommy once when I was a baby. May daddy calls her my tummy mummy. But now that you're here he says you're a bit like my second mommy," Helen blushed vividly and began to shovel food back in her mouth as she stared at the plate nervously.

Amanda reeled at what she heard. Terrence thinks of her as a kind of mother to Helen? It was a loving thought that warmed her but at the same time…. What did that mean exactly? Did he see her as a surrogate wife? Part of her hoped so. She leaned forward and touched Helen's hair and smiled.

"I'm not your mommy Helen but I really wish I was,"

And the little girl smiled with chubby, chicken filled cheeks.

~

After dinner the two girls settled down in the living room with pencils and paper and Amanda watched happily as Helen doodled.

"And what's that?"

"This is a puppy!" Helen beamed and shoved the paper in Amanda's face.

"It's lovely! And you like puppies?"

"I LOVE puppies! One day I'm going to have a hundred of them," Helen smiled to herself and carried on drawing.

"That's so nice," Amanda said a little half-heartedly.

Her mind was still on the sheriff and she couldn't get silly thoughts out of her head. Part of her felt like some sort of usurper that had blustered into the family and taken Evangeline's place but the other part of her relished the thought.

A moment later the front door rattled and the steady sound of the sheriff's boots was heard entering the house.

"Daddy!" Helen ran to her father. "I drew puppies!"

Terrence picked her up and looked at her drawing as if he was trying to decipher a code.

"That's just great kid, really great," he said unconvincingly before putting her back down and rubbing his tired eyes.

"But Daddy look! Puppies!" Helen was adamant that her father find her drawings to be masterpieces.

Terrence looked to Amanda with desperate eyes and the governess took the hint.

"Come on pumpkin let's get you ready for bed,"

"Thanks," the sheriff sighed and rubbed his brow.

After putting an incredibly grumpy little princess to bed Helen joined her boss out on the porch with a tumbler of whiskey.

"So you're getting a liking for the stuff?" Terrence nodded at her glass.

"Eh…yeah! Kinda," she swallowed a mouthful and winced as it hit the back of her throat. She didn't really like it she just wanted to look like an adult and be closer to Terrence in some way.

"Good stuff," Terrence knocked back his entire glass in one go.

The truth was that they were both so nervous around each other that most of the time they could barely communicate without a shot of Dutch courage.

"But don't get likin' it too much," said the sheriff. "Or you'll grow old before your time, like me….."

Amanda sensed a deep sadness coming from the man and she so badly wanted to wrap an arm around him to comfort him, make him feel ok. The longer the young girl had spent in the house the more she realized the sheriff was a simmering pot of unresolved issues. She just wished she could help.

"So how was work?" she changed the subject quickly.

"Urgh…. Just my usual weekend constitutional," he laughed to himself.

"Oh no! Not the Colt again?" Amanda laughed.

"Don't even get me started!"

Jimmy "Colt" Carson was a nightmare in Wattsville and caused havoc wherever he went. The local bruiser and, fortunately for him, the nephew of the mayor, he came from a rich family and he let everyone know it. Due to his stature and family ties he loved the fact that he had free reign on the town but there was always that one person whom he couldn't conquer. The sheriff hated him and welcomed every chance to arrest him. Over the last ten years they'd been stuck in a power struggle that the sheriff only won but Colt was too stupid to realize. Now every time Friday night rolled round and the boy had a drink too many he'd find himself in the cells. Not that he'd care though because like clockwork his father would come round and bail him out within the hour. But the sheriff had noticed that over the last few weeks he'd started to take his time getting to the station. He smirked to himself as he thought that even the boy's family were tiring of his shenanigans.

"Well at least that kid keeps me in shape!" the sheriff laughed.

"That's true. I think he's kinda sad though," Amanda as always was the compassionate one. "I mean every week now I've been watching him… I think he's rather lost."

"You think too much," Terrence said gruffly and looked to the stars as he sat awkwardly.

But his awkwardness turned to butterflies as he sensed the warmth of her soft fingers on his arm. He looked to see Amanda edging towards him with a concerned look on her face.

"I think you're rather lost too sometimes…" she whispered as she got closer.

Amanda rested her head on his shoulder knowing there was a chance the sheriff would reject her and she'd be embarrassed beyond all comprehension. Yet at the same time she longed to comfort him and make everything ok. Terrence leaned into her and she felt the heat between them. She wanted those strong arms around her as they kissed each other.

Meanwhile the sheriff had never felt so conflicted. He wanted to grab her here and now and push her down onto the ground but he knew he couldn't because that darkness was seething inside of him, that guilt that came from feeling desire. He leaned into her and smelled the fresh and florid scent of her hair mixed with the warmth of her skin. For a moment he wondered if he should kiss her and he bent down to meet her lips. Yet as he felt the electricity between them he felt like a dangerous man. He wasn't sure what he could be capable of if he was to lose control of his urges. Terrence quickly pulled away and stood up.

"I have to go check on Helen," he lied and hurried into the house.

Amanda felt humiliated but even more desperate for him to love her. She looked down to her empty glass and wished it was full.

CHAPTER 9

As the morning rolled around the sheriff woke up groggily but was eager to get down to the station. If, like last week, that idiot Colt was still in the cells he was going to go to town on him. He needed that release, that expenditure of negative energy that could only come from harsh physical activity.

His stroll down to the station was a nervous one. Terrence was panicking that he'd passed up a chance with Amanda, they he'd made a fool of himself. He looked back to the house and saw the soft figure of the girl in the downstairs window staring wistfully after him. Maybe he did still have a chance. Urgh....but that was the problem! He cursed himself for the hundredth time for finding her attractive. How easy his life would be if she were ugly and obnoxious. Some friends had suggested he fire her to solve his problem, to send her packing back to Boston with no explanation whatsoever. But he just couldn't because Helen would be distraught and of course… so would he.

He heard Tony's laughter before he saw it and as he entered the station he saw his deputy standing jovially with Colt's father, a refined looking gentleman who had aged beyond his years. The two turned to the sheriff when they heard the authoritative noise of his boots.

"Morning sir," Colt's father lifted off his hat and bowed a little too formally.

"Good day Mr Carson. I assume you're here to collect little Jimmy?" he reached out and shook the old man's hand.

"Urgh… that little toad can stay right here where he belongs," Mr Carson laughed. "He needs to learn his lesson this time. Keep him as long as you want."

"Are you sure?" Terrence wasn't certain he'd heard correctly.

"Oh yeah absolutely you have my blessing. Fed up of hauling his sorry ass out of here every weekend like my life's not hard enough already," he rolled his eyes and grunted.

"Very well… He'll be a common prisoner for the remainder of the week," Terrence smiled with insidious thoughts lighting up his eyes.

"Well… fair well sheriff, I trust you to see that my son learns a lesson," and the old man jauntily placed his hat back on his head and sauntered out the building.

"Think he's finally given up on the Colt?" Tony asked with hope in his voice.

"Yup…sure seems it," Terrence twitched his lips into a little sly smile that only Tony would recognize as a sign of danger.

His deputy got the hint.

"Well why don't you head down there and see that he learns that lesson," he encouraged his boss.

Terrence walked purposely into the basement with no hesitation and shouted behind him:

"Keep yourself busy! I may be some time," his hard boots hit off the stone steps that told the prisoners there was trouble coming.

Terrence could smell that fearful sweat coming off the wretches as they cowered in their cells. He could swear he heard their breathing as it accelerated and as he scanned the cells he could practically hear their thoughts.

'Please…don't pick me…' their eyes pleaded but they had nothing to worry about because the sheriff only had eyes for Colt. His cell was at the end of the line and over the past few years it had almost been exclusively his. He often joked to his friends that he was staying in the Wattsville Hilton for the weekend and he even started leaving some of his belongings in there over the week. Sundries were piled next to the bleak mattress on the floor and Colt even had a spare pair of shoes in there in case he had to go straight from jail to work. As he saw the sheriff approaching he started to pace the floor like a caged animal. His enormous body seemed to fill the entire space both with muscles and presence but Terrence wasn't afraid. He knew the boy was as dumb as a bag of wet mice and a lousy fighter too despite his size. All that boozing and gratuitous living was starting to take its toll on his body and he'd often sit on the ground wheezing after only throwing one punch, not that he was smart enough to back down though.

"This time sheriff you're mine!" he attempted to say menacingly through the bars.

"Pffffff….. get a new line," Terrence laughed. He'd heard his empty threats every week for years.

"I mean it this time! My dad will be here any second and he'll have your ass on a plate,"

"Your dear father was in my office not even a minute ago and he doesn't give a shit about you. Says he's leavin' you here to rot; under MY watch."

"You're lyin'! Don't you lie to me sheriff!" Colt started to rattle in his cage with anger but he knew that deep down Terrence was telling the truth. He'd often seen the humiliation in his father's eyes and knew this time would come.

Terrence could see the hesitation on his face and that fear pop up with a look of betrayal.

"You better start prayin'," Terrence spoke very slowly through gritted teeth as he unbuckled his belt.

"Why? You wanna fuck me pretty boy?" Colt joked. "I ain't no beautiful Boston belle now am I?" he shot Terrence a cunning look.

"What did you say?" Terrence got even angrier as he pulled the belt from its loops.

"What? You think no one knows? That you've been wanting that sweet little governess' pussy? Well you want some news? I've had her and she was just beautiful…." the boy smiled to show his vulgar gold tooth that reigned over the rest.

"What did you say?" Terrence gripped Colt's shirt through the bars and pulled him close.

"You heard me sheriff. Once when you were workin' late I headed over to your place and she welcomed me with open arms, or should I saw open legs? She even fried me up a steak after," he chuckled as he pretended to remember.

"You son of a bitch! You're lying!" and the sheriff quickly fumbled for his keys to open the cell.

Colt meanwhile was pretending to be scared when in fact he genuinely was. He lifted up his hands and mimicked a girl's voice.

"Oh sheriff are you not even gonna take me out first? You know flowers wouldn't hurt either," he pouted.

Terrence quickly shot his knuckles straight into Colt's face and blood immediately started streaming from his nose. He fell back on his backside with a childish look of shock on his face. Terrence half expected him to burst into tears like a baby but instead the boy just sat their stunned.

"You wanna tell me more about you and the governess?" Terrence goaded.

Colt though just shook his head in fear of further consequences.

"Good. Now get up,"

Colt was still stunned and clutched at his face as blood ran into this mouth and coated his teeth.

"I SAID GET THE FUCK UP!"

The boy jumped up from the floor as if taking orders.

"You boy are gonna fight me properly. If you win I'll set you free immediately and you can run your sorry ass back to your father's with your tail between your legs. But if you lose I get to keep you here… until you do win."

It seemed like a completely fair game to the sheriff and Colt was too stupid to think otherwise. Not that he had an option anyway.

"It's a deal," the boy said with intention in his voice. "I'm gonna make sure you're so ruined you'll have to leave this town for good,"

"So you keep sayin'," smiled the sheriff.

The men circled each other within the walls of the narrow cell in a peculiar dance of machismo. Terrence looked primed and ready, with adrenaline pumping so violently through him he was ready to burst. His brow already dropped beads of sweat and he held up his fists as though he believed they were made from solid rock. Colt however acted like his hands were made of hams and he fumbled with his fists as though he wasn't quite sure what to do with them.

Terrence landed the first punch, right in the side of Colt's head. It seemed to do nothing to the boy's confidence though and he took it without flinching as if it made no impact. It was Colt's turn next and as he attempted to plough his fist into the center of the sheriff's face he quickly dodged it and retaliated with a mighty blow straight into the boy's gut. Colt landed back on his behind winded and in terrible pain.

"You lose again kid," laughed the sheriff.

Terrence then picked up his belt that he'd hung between the bars. He wrapped one end around his hand and let the buckle end hang loose and deadly like a viper's tail. Colt saw the glint of the metal and his eyes grew wide in fear.

"No….Now what?" he stuttered.

"Now we begin," Terrence spoke menacingly.

"You're crazy! You've gone fucking bat shit crazy,"

"Don't you know it," was all the sheriff said before he lost control of his mind.

He whipped the belt hitting Colt in the arm who looked down to see blood running from an open wound on his bicep.

"What the hell man? You've lost it!"

But the sheriff wasn't listening. He was lost in his own sordid reverie as he tried to relieve his own pain.

Upstairs Tony was certain he heard the screams of Colt but who was he to check up on his boss? He nervously sat quietly in his chair and lit a cigarette.

CHAPTER 10

Dinner time came and Amanda sat with Helen in the kitchen having an in depth conversation about what the world would look like if all humans were replaced with puppies and kittens.

"And I'd be their princess! But I would be a nice one and they could just do what they wanted!"

"Uhuh… So would you have a prince to help you run your adorable kingdom?" Amanda asked but she had her eyes on the clock and didn't much care for the answer.

"Eeeeuww! No! Boys are stinky. It would just be me and my animals," Helen nodded to signal she'd made a very important decision.

"You're a very clever girl," Amanda kissed the girl on the cheek and her little face beamed.

"Can I have more biscuits and gravy please?"

"Of course my little pumpkin!" Amanda was thrilled.

Before the governess' arrival the little girl ate like a sparrow and despised everything her father made her. Terrence had loved watching his daughter grow up over the last year into a healthy and bouncy girl instead of a listless and grumpy one.

"When's daddy home?" Helen asked as she mopped up some gravy with a biscuit.

"Hmmmm… I don't know. He should have been home half an hour ago," Amanda looked at the clock again.

After dinner the little girl quietly and dutifully headed up to her bedroom to play insisting she had "girly work" to do. Amanda checked in on her and saw that she had an array of soft toys lined up on her bed while she gave a little speech about how she'd give them a better life with kibbles made of sparkly chocolate. Amanda smiled and closed the bedroom door.

It was now late and the sheriff still hadn't come home. The governess thought to herself that if the house were to be robbed the last thing to be taken would be the clock because she was watching it so intently. She felt like a housewife waiting for her drunken husband to come home and guilt swept over her. Who was she to care about when her boss was home? She tried to keep the sheriff out of her mind but the more she tried to busy herself with chores the more she wondered where he was. He was never late and always loved coming home to Helen.

"Maybe he's been hurt at work," she whispered to herself as she scrubbed the floor. "That'll be it. Or maybe he just has a lot to do at the station."

But bedtime for Helen came and went and there was still no sign of the sheriff. Butterflies were rampant in the governess' tummy and now she stood in the darkness of the living room. She made another quick glance at the clock and sighed.

The governess resigned herself to bed with great sadness. Her happiest time of the day had been and gone. She lay awake for hours, staring at the ceiling feeling ridiculous and naïve. He wasn't her husband and where he was shouldn't concern her. But in the back of her mind something was niggling at her. The more she tried to shake it away the more it came back. She pulled the covers up over her head hoping that the complete darkness would suffocate her anxiety.

Just as sleep came to her she was startled into alertness. The front door! It was opening and then the familiar sound of those hard boots was heard pacing the floorboards. However there seemed to be an unusual spring in the sheriff's step and as he ascended the stairs he did something he'd never done before. He began to whistle. Amanda was now more anxious than ever and as she tried to sleep she felt the illogical compulsion to cross her fingers for luck.

"Please may he have not been with another woman," she repeated to herself like a mantra.

~

Birds chirped outside of Amanda's window and for a brief second she thought she was back at home with her family. That was until she heard the pitter patter of little feet running up the hallway and stopping at her door. A tiny rapping sounded before the door creaked open.

"Miss Amanda?" the little voice said. "Good morning Miss Amanda! Can I have cake for breakfast? My daddy said I could have cake," Helen tried to convince her governess.

"Are you sure about that?" Amanda laughed.

Helen nodded with her thumb in her mouth and climbed up onto her governess' bed. This had become a new habit of hers and although Amanda thought it adorable she worried the little girl was becoming too attached to her. She gently put the girl back down on the floor.

"Don't get too comfortable, you have to get dressed and brush your hair," she tried to say with at least some authority.

The little girl huffed and walked away scuffing her feet. As Amanda got dressed and headed downstairs she heard that noise again, happy whistling. As she entered the kitchen she saw the sheriff look happier than he had since her arrival. A big smile swept across his face.

"Morning girls!" he sang as he saw Amanda bring his daughter downstairs. "What's this about us having cake for breakfast? Sounds like a marvellous idea!" and he scooped up a giggling Helen.

"You've changed…" Amanda meant to sound happy and friendly but the words came out sounding suspicious.

"Haha! It's just this lovely weather we're having. I can feel the spring comin' on the breeze,"

Amanda wasn't convinced.

"You were home late last night. Helen and I waited up for you, didn't we?" she asked the little girl who looked somewhat baffled but nodded anyway.

"Late night at the station," was all he said and he resumed his whistling.

Amanda had a knot in her stomach and it embarrassed her. She felt like a jealous wife and that made her sad because she knew that wasn't what the sheriff found attractive. He liked strong dependable woman who could take care of themselves. She looked up to his face and saw a newly gained sparkle that shone in his eyes. He'd definitely had sex last night no doubt about it. A man was never so happy over anything else.

"So…. You make any new friends last night?" Amanda prodded for answers and immediately regretted her ridiculously transparent question.

"Well isn't that an odd thing to ask? I didn't realize governesses had a right to ask about their employers' social lives," his tone was acidic but he didn't mean it to be. "I mean… It's not like you're usually interested in this sort of thing," he said a little softer.

The two looked to each other with faces that begged for more information. They both wanted to sit down and resolve the elephant in the room but decorum can be a terrible thing. They didn't say another word again and eventually the sheriff left for work. Amanda watched him longingly from the porch as he left. Meanwhile Terrence had a feeling deep in his gut that things were coming to a head. The tension in the house couldn't continue and he felt he was getting closer and closer to accepting her invitation of an open door at night.

This morning the sheriff wasn't going to the station and so his usual habit of strolling to work would be broken. Rather he walked to the stable at the back of his property and grabbed his horse Betsy by the reigns.

"There's ma girl!" he kissed her on the nose and patted the top of her head. "Miss me did ya?"

He pulled her from the stable and jumped up on the saddle. It felt good to be high up and especially as he rarely got the opportunity to ride the old girl much anymore.

"I promise after today I'm gonna take you out more," he said to his dusty, brown horse that he'd cared for longer than his own daughter.

She was in fact Evangeline's horse and whenever he saw the stables he would often imagine his wife cantering elegantly through the trees. Her auburn hair would fly wildly behind her like a cape and her soft feminine face would look regal. He missed her so much and as he looked down to the horse he felt that she was one of very few final connections to the lady he pledged his life too.

He rode down the dirt track to some cornfields that lay on the outskirts of the town, big breezy plots of land that seldom saw people unless they were in trouble. Over the centuries stories had circulated through the generations of witches having been hung in these fields but the sheriff thought that was garbage; just parents trying to scare their kids so they wouldn't run away too far from home. But he had to admit to himself, the fields could become eerie at times. The wind would rustle through the corn right up to your ear and make sounds that sounded like whispers. The monotonous landscape of identical plants often made it look like you were walking through an optical illusion. At times the corn would mutate into shapes in your mind and you'd see things flash at the corners of your eyes. Shadow people would flitter back and forth between the liminal spaces of your blind spots and vision. Terrence shivered on the saddle as he arrived at the edge of the biggest field. Those things were just tricks of the mind! Or so he told himself anyway.

"Easy girl," he patted Betsy on the head to calm her down as she walked through the high corn. She never was any good at riding into places she'd never been before.

She soon relaxed and walked at a steady pace. All that could be heard was the sound of corn husks rubbing off the sides of the horse and to Terrence it sounded like the sea. He sure would like to see the sea again someday. He imagined that Amanda would have been to the beach as a child and frolicked in the waves having been born in Boston. He thought of the young governess getting wet in the ocean and he had to calm himself. He lightly slapped his cheeks with his hands and tried to focus on the task at hand. Somewhere around him he could hear the sound of shackles and he pulled at the reigns to stop Betsy. He was nearly at the spot.

"I can hear ya! Ya dumb prick," the arrogant voice drifted over the corn to Terrence's ears.

"I can year you too you idiot!" the sheriff retorted as he jumped down from his horse.

He followed the sound of his shackles until he reached an opening in the corn that he had made the previous night. Sitting on the ground with a dried and weathered face sat Colt. His skin was crusted in blood and his eyes were swollen but despite this he still remained as obtuse and full of himself as ever.

"So ya thought you'd come back and finish the job," he asked more than he declared. There was barely an ounce of fear in his voice anymore and the sheriff had surmised that the kid had given up.

"You don't sound like your whiny little bitch self," the sheriff kicked at the shackles threateningly.

"Oh yeah, well I got a reason for that! You left me out here to die but I looked up to those stars for hours and they spoke to me. I found God last night and he told me everything was gonna be ok. If you hurt me again I'll go to heaven and that suits me fine," he was rambling.

"You've lost it kid. One night off the liquor and you think you've seen God," Terrence laughed and shook his head.

"But don't worry I ain't here to kill ya. Who would I have to beat up every weekend if you weren't around as my personal punching bag?"

"You're a sick man sheriff! When my father finds out about this he'll have your balls in a vice!" Colt tried to remain angry and menacing but he was tiring.

"Yeah your father…. The one who gave me permission to beat your ass," Terrence left that fact hanging in the air solemnly. "He's given up on ya kid!" he kicked at the shackles again.

"So what then… What are you gonna do to me?" Colt was genuinely worried and wanted to know. If he wasn't to die then what?

"Just you wait and see," was all the sheriff said before he walked back to his horse.

CHAPTER 11

Amanda was putting the finishing touches to Helen's hair and as she looked over the little princess she was proud of herself. As always the girl looked like a porcelain doll.

"Say Helen…. Would you fancy doing something a little different today?"

The little girl turned up her big beautiful eyelashes that framed the bluest of eyes.

"Something different?" she pondered the idea for a while then eventually grinned. "Sure!"

"Great! But can you promise me something?"

Again the girl nodded but this time conspiratorially.

"Can you keep this a secret between just you and me? I'm afraid your daddy wouldn't understand super-secret girl business,"

Helen found this hilarious and wrapped her tiny arms around the governess in glee.

"Is it super-secret princess business?" she asked.

"It is! And no one can know about it. Do we have a deal?"

Helen reached out her little hand and the two girls shook on it.

~

Having walked Helen through the neighbouring fields the girls arrived at a nearby house. It was bigger than the sheriff's but musty and old. Amanda always thought that a gust of wind could take it away in a moment but as ever she saw it standing as proudly as it always had. An old woman with grey hair wrapped up in a severe bun sat on the porch cleaning her teeth with an ivory tooth pick. She pulled the pick from between her teeth and inspected it as if it might have produced gold. She placed it back into her mouth and rocked back on her chair.

"Mrs Wheen?" Amanda's soft voice surprised the old lady who looked over the field startled.

"Who is it? Amanda is that you? I haven't got my glasses on!" she shouted although she didn't need to.

"Yes it's me Mrs Wheen," said the governess from a few feet away.

"Oh lovely! And is that precious little girl with you today?"

"Good morning Mrs Wheen!" Helen's tiny, cheerful voice brought sunshine to the old lady's face.

Helen jumped up on Mrs Wheen's lap and kissed her cheek.

"We have secret princess business today," Helen said as if it was normal.

"We do?" Mrs Wheen asked a little confused.

"If you don't mind," interrupted Amanda. "I have an errand to run for an hour or so, would you be so kind as to mind Helen?"

"Well of course! What a delight!"

"And one last thing…. May I borrow that horse of yours?"

~

Amanda had definitely heard Terrence leave with Betsy but where was he going? Certainly not the station… so what was he up to? She looked at the tracks on the dirt path and was pleased to see that no wind had blown them away. If she hurried she might be able to trace them all the way to where the sheriff was.

She wasn't used to riding horses and thought the concept rather odd to be sitting on an animal's back while it took you places. Nevertheless she felt comfortable on the old mare that was Mrs Wheen's horse Mathilda. She was a devoted and slow thing with big soft eyes and indiscriminate tufts of hair and as she took her from the stable she vowed to take care of her. But now that she was making her way out of town she prayed that the old girl would hurry the hell up.

As Amanda got further and further from the house and from Helen she felt terrible. What was she doing? Spying on her boss? She felt as though she was going crazy and knew that the logical thing to do was to turn around and forget all this business… but she couldn't. Her mind was running wild. She looked out into the corn fields in the distance and imagined him out there in a lover's embrace with a girl much prettier than herself. In fact she imagined a whole array of scenarios that all ended in heartbreak for her. And what was she meant to do once she found him? Declare her love for him and send him home. Ridiculous… She felt as though she was acting like a lovesick buffoon.

Soon enough though the hoof marks on the track appeared to be turning into one of the fields. She looked over to see a big tunnel through the corn that had been recently carved out. Following it down she tried her best to keep Mathilda quiet although her age could be heard loudly with her constant snuffling and wheezing.

"Quiet girl… Please. I promise there'll be lots of sugar cubes and carrots when I take you home if you just shut up for a second," she said as though it were possible that her words would make a difference.

Suddenly a noise caught Amanda's attention and it stopped her dead in her tracks. She leapt down from the horse and crouched amongst the corn to hide. It was the sound of someone in pain she thought…. Or was it the amorous sounds of love making? Her paranoia meant that she couldn't be sure unless she saw it with her own eyes.

She was practically on all fours as she shuffled through the corn to get closer to the source of the noise. She was scared that at any minute she'd stumble upon some awful scene and she'd either be in danger or terribly embarrassed. But there was that sound again and this time it was louder. It was definitely someone in pain, a man perhaps. Something else accompanied it. A noise that sounded like the air was being sliced open and Amanda recognised it as the sound of a belt flying through the air at speed. She could recognise it in an instant because it was the same sound her maths teacher's belt made when she was caught talking in the back of the classroom. It immediately brought her back to being a fourteen year old girl and that sense of mischief flooded her again.

The noise felt closer and now she could make out a few words as they painfully escaped the mouth of an unknown man.

"Sheriff no! You've lost your damn mind!" the voice echoed.

So Terrence WAS here! What was he doing? Amanda didn't have to wonder for long because as she pulled back the long leaves of the corn the scene unveiled itself. The sheriff was beating Colt senseless with the buckle end of a belt. The young man was bloody and distressed with swollen eyes and open wounds on his skin. Amanda shrunk back into the plants and gasped. She couldn't quite believe what she was seeing, she was terrified. What if Terrence found her out here spying on him? Would he brutalize her too?

The niggling inside her was there again and she couldn't shake it off. Every time she heard the crack of the whip it made her heart thump, her breathing shallow and… it made her tremendously wet. She peeked back out into the clearing and watched the violent spectacle again but this time she took her eyes off Colt and kept them fixed on Terrence.

His arms were flexing with his muscles bulging through his shirt. Sweat glistened on his brow and Amanda traced the beads of moisture as they trickled down the sides of his face and down his neck. She imagined being close to him and smelling that sweat, feeling the heat rise from his body as she reached out a hand to stroke his muscular chest. She'd feel that wetness through his shirt and leaning in she'd flick her tongue across the delicate skin of his neck and lick hungrily.

Amanda pushed her hand up under her petticoats and found the hot wetness between her legs. She pushed a finger inside and rubbed her clitoris with the palm of her hand. She listened to the belt again.

CRACK!

"Urgh…." She bit her lip and felt herself close already.

CRACK!

She loved to watch that power in Terrence as she tried her hardest not to scream.

CRACK!

She was riding her hand now, bouncing up and down pushing herself onto her fingers. Looking out through the leaves she gazed over every part of the sheriff's body as he grew tired. But he hadn't lost any of that anger, he whipped one last time.

CRACK!

And Amanda shuddered violently as she contracted around her fingers in the best orgasm she'd ever had. Shaking uncontrollably she clenched her eyes shut and tried to supress the loud gasps of pleasure she wanted to make. As she came she fell forward on her front. She breathed in the earthen scent of the ground as her face lay on the soil. Her eyes though could see through a gap in the plants and she looked on lovingly at the shackles. She wanted to be restrained by them so badly so Terrence could be in control of her too.

CHAPTER 12

Amanda had crashed into bed with thoughts swirling in her mind. A mix of guilt and pleasure flooded her body as she tried to sleep. *I can't believe I got turned on by someone's pain*, she thought to herself. She felt like a dreadful person but at the same time it wasn't Colt she was aroused over it was the dominance. It was the sheriff with his dangerous anger, his violent temper and the god damn sound of that whip that got her fired up.

Of course she kept her lips sealed though when Terrence had returned home. After her earlier indiscretion she had scurried away from the field terrified of being caught and quickly hurried home. By some sort of miracle she had remained unseen and she was very grateful. She was certain however that the sheriff had noticed that mischievous glint in her eyes that gave away her secret. But maybe that was her paranoia again.

She tossed and turned in her bed but couldn't sleep. Nothing felt right anymore except the harsh domination she desired from the sheriff. For the thousandth time she wondered if she should go down to his bedroom and present herself. Over the months she'd thought of dozens of ways of doing it; crawling in naked on all fours with a sliver of rope between her teeth like an obedient dog or calling him into her bedroom where she would lay wearing nothing but a blindfold.

"Bring over those cuffs," she'd purr seductively and finally he'd hold her down and push himself into her.

But her desire was only surpassed by her tremendous shyness and so each night Amanda lay in bed unable to sleep thinking of what it would be like to feel a little braver.

~

Terrence lay on top of his covers to cool down and gazed out of the window at the stars. The moon was shining into the bedroom illuminating his body as it lay exhausted. He'd managed somehow to catch himself with the belt a few times and he looked down at the cuts on his arms and legs. He hoped that no one would notice but what did he care anyway? He thought back to earlier in the day and perused his mind for his favourite memories. Of course seeing the fear in Colt's eyes as he realized he wasn't boss anymore was at the top spot. But he also tried to emotionally grasp hold of that sense of power in his mind, that satisfaction that came from owning a human like a dog even if it was just for a little while.

He noticed again this evening that Amanda had left her door open and he wondered what it would be like to hold her body as if it was his. He imagined owning her curves and breasts, of having her beautiful face just for himself and of course pleasuring himself with her over and over again. He wanted her to be his personal toy and as his eyes looked out to the hallway he wondered whether he should walk down there naked and pull back her covers. He'd be gentle at first, caressing her breasts and kissing her softly but then he'd show his masculinity and she would melt beneath him as she relented under his hard body. She'd open up to him and want more and more until he had nothing left to give except for his love.

What can I do to have her? He thought to himself as he looked at the moon shining on his bed. His gaze followed the beam of light until it reached his bedside table and he saw the face of Evangeline. *Fuck, what am I even thinking?* He thought as he picked up the framed photo of his wife. He kissed it as he had many times before and lay it back down.

~

"So…..where's the bad boy?" Tony inquired about Colt the following morning.

"Oh…I took care of him," the sheriff said glibly.

"Well that doesn't sound good boss! Is he ok?"

"Believe me… he's better where he is," the reply came ominously.

Of course the sheriff hadn't actually done anything so terrible with him despite Tony's worrying and constant beard twiddling. He had in fact dragged the boy home to his father and demanded that he be removed from the town. His father, eager to teach the boy a lesson had agreed and began making plans for him to live with his strict and highly religious grandfather out of state.

"He's alive though ain't he?" Tony asked a little frightened.

"Yeah but he's gonna wish he wasn't," Terrence laughed at the thought of the dumb kid being disciplined by his grandpa.

He sat down at his desk and sparked a cigarette, exhaling blue smoke out into the bull pen of the station.

"Ever thought of giving those up?" asked the deputy.

"Never," the sheriff said defiantly. "They keep me from losin' my mind…. But anyway…It's sure quiet in here without that kid,"

"Yup," Tony leaned back in his chair bored and looked up to the ceiling as if it would entertain him. "That boy was like ninety percent of this town's crime rate," he laughed.

"I think there's maybe still some drunks down in the cells if you're looking for something to do," Terrence suggested.

"Nah!" Tony laughed and began lighting matches and watching them burn for a few seconds before blowing them out and throwing them away. "So you and the governess girl, has it happened yet?"

"I don't know what you're insinuating deputy," Terrence lied.

"Don't give me your nonsense sheriff you know what I mean,"

Terrence thought deeply for a minute and placed his fingers together, holding them to his chin. He was choosing his words carefully, paying close attention to not make himself sound like a lovesick teenager but it was useless.

"Oh God Tony she drives me wild!"

"Ha! What have I been tellin' ya, you gotta go for it!"

"I just can't…. it wouldn't be fair on Helen,"

"You know full well that ain't true! It would be the BEST thing for your little girl," Tony explained.

"Well you got me there," Terrence knew his deputy was right.

He shoved his head into the palms of his hands and lay forward on his desk. He thought that with time his lust for her would dissipate but of course it never did, it only got stronger. Every moment in the house with her was a tension riddled feat of temptation. Maybe tonight he'd do it. He'd just grab hold of her and kiss her hard, and he knew that she wanted him too. He wasn't stupid after all and had noticed all those pouty, sultry looks she gave him over the dinner table. The sheriff ran scenarios through his mind of what he would do but each time his mind would got to dark places and he reigned his thoughts back in.

The clickety clop of lady's heels was heard softly coming up the station steps and Tony hurried out to the door. He was grateful just to have something to do and he eagerly greeted the person on the stairs. Terrence however wondered who it could be because he'd never seen a grin so wide on his deputy's face before.

"You've got a special guest sheriff," he beamed.

The rustle of skirts shimmied in through the doorway and Terrence looked the woman in front of him up and down with awe. He thought she looked more beautiful than ever.

"Can I speak with you in private sheriff?" Amanda's dainty voice sounded desperate and sad. "Something terrible has happened!"

"Oh! Of course! Of course! Is Helen ok?"

"Yes she's ok. I took the liberty of putting her in the care of Mrs Wheen," she nodded to insist she'd done the right thing.

"Well please, this way immediately," Terrence showed the girl downstairs in a hurry. "So what's the matter? What's happened?"

Now that the two were in the basement Amanda could speak freely and she looked around the dingy room to make sure she was speaking in private. All she could see were two sleeping drunk vagrants in a cell at the end but the others were empty. She quickly grabbed Terrence's hand and pulled him into one of the cells and slammed the barred gate behind her.

"Sheriff you have to listen! I have to tell you something really important!"

"What the hell is going on Amanda?" Terrence was completely baffled.

"Sheriff…..I've been a very bad girl,"

~

The night had been long and Amanda couldn't shake away the memory of the sheriff in the corn field. He had just looked so powerful and manly, like he came from a more archaic time when men were more beast than gentleman. Every time she thought of his wide stance and huge biceps she felt herself grow wet and she'd have to rub herself on whatever was near; the inside of her panties, the hardness of her chair, the soft skin of her hand. There must be something she could do to provoke him into bed without making a fool of herself. Maybe if she did something really bad he'd get angry enough to punish her. She entertained the thought for a long while and in the midst of her constant arousal it seemed to make sense.

She went upstairs and into Terrence's bedroom. A private place she had never freely walked in before. Amanda immediately felt guilty as though she was trespassing on forbidden territory but her guilt turned to concern when she saw that the sheriff lived so spartanly. There was hardly any furniture, despite the size of the room, and there were hardly any personal touches. Amanda gathered that all those things left the moment his wife did and she felt terribly sad. But the sadness gave her an idea and as she looked to the bedside table she saw the beautiful portrait of Evangeline. She sauntered over and ever so gracefully bashed into the side of the bedside table. The photograph went tumbling to the ground with its protective glass smashing into pieces.

"That'll do it!" Amanda said triumphantly to herself.

Now that the deed was done the governess wasted no time in setting her plan into action. She hurried Helen over to Mrs Wheen's and quickly ran down to the station. As always Tony was ecstatic to see her and smiled that big grin of his. She had often wondered at times whether she should cut her losses and settle down with Tony. She knew he liked her and he was single after all. But she just couldn't because she only had eyes for that burly sheriff of hers.

As she entered the station she saw Terrence rise from his desk looking startled to see her and of course he would be, she had never set foot in the station since she arrived in Wyoming. She acted in peril as best as she could and was thrilled when he took her down to the cells. It was exactly where she wanted him.

"I've been a very bad girl," she blurted out as sexily as she could and looked at him in awe as he responded.

She looked down to see the bulge in his pants and knew she'd done the right thing. She wanted to reach her hand out and grip him hard but she waited for him to take the lead.

"What did you do?" Terrence asked her with suspicion in his eyes.

"I thought I'd be kind and clean your bedroom for you and I started to dust your bedside table..." she trailed off.

Terrence's eyes grew wide.

"But the feather duster caught the side of that beautiful photograph of yours and well...." she spoke in a baby voice and tried to look as small as possible.

"And well what?"

"This..." Amanda pulled the broken wreckage from her pocket and showed it to him. "The photograph is still ok, it's just the glass," she pouted.

But the anger was rising in the sheriff and storm clouds seemed to come over his eyes. He felt the compulsion to ring Amanda by her neck. How dare she touch Evangeline's beautiful portrait? But if was just an accident?

"You should NEVER have been in there!" he shouted.

"I know, I know! I'm so sorry. I won't do it again I promise," Amanda cried as she worried she had pushed him too far and he now hated her.

But the sheriff slumped as he looked down to the broken glass.

"I guess we can fix this though, it's just the glass right?"

Amanda nodded.

"But aren't you going to punish me?" she was pushing her luck now.

"What are you? A school girl?" he asked jokingly but he desperately hoped that she'd nod and bend over demanding to be spanked.

"I was a very naughty girl sheriff and I deserve to be punished," she pouted again.

The bulge in the sheriff's pants grew bigger and Amanda looked down and desperately wanted to wrap her mouth around it.

"And how do you suggest I punish you?" Terrence started to play along.

"I need spanked sheriff…hard," Amanda noticed the glint in his eyes and knew the time was right, she was all his.

"Well come here then!" Terrence ordered and sat down on the harsh wooden bench of the cell. "Bend over!" he shouted.

Without any hesitation Amanda bent over his knee and bit her lip. Just one slap would drive her crazy and she waited with baited breath. She felt his fingers start to tickle the back of her calf as he rose up her petticoats.

"You know….." he paused. "Little girls who misbehave deserve to be severely punished. Wouldn't you agree?"

"Oh yes sheriff!" she nodded eagerly, desperate to please him.

"Good. I think so too," and Terrence pulled up her skirt so that her bottom was now showing with its delicate covering of white lace. "Such pretty little panties for such a bad girl," he said as he pulled them down roughly. "Bad girls don't deserve such cute things," he said aggressively as he rose up his hand ready to strike. "Are you ready for your spanking?"

"Yes sheriff!" Amanda begged.

And in one swift motion Terrence smacked the palm of his hand down onto her pale skin and hit her hard. The sounds of skin on skin echoed in the basement and Amanda screamed in pleasure as the pain hit her.

"Aaaaaaah!" she yelped in a mix of agony and ecstasy.

Meanwhile Terrence had never felt so aroused. He finally had the governess where he wanted her and looked down to the girl on his lap and felt intensely pleased with himself.

"You've been a terrible girl Amanda! You should never enter my room without my permission!" he slapped her again and grew harder as he watched a pinkness spread across her white bottom.

"I'm so sorry sheriff! I promise I'll be good!" she pleaded.

"And you should never touch my things!" he slapped her again and she screamed even louder.

He felt his bulge press against the heat of her body and he felt the desperate need to rub himself against her. The pressure against his pants was enough to make him feel close to orgasm and he pulled away to stop himself.

"Now stand up!" he ordered.

Amanda jumped up and did as she was told with a smile on her face.

"Take off your clothes," he said sternly. "Now it's time for your real punishment,"

Amanda dutifully pulled her dress and corset down and stood naked in the cell. She had never felt so vulnerable before and she stood in the basement with only the bars of the cells to hide her modesty.

"Now sit down there!" Terrence shouted and pointed to the ground.

Amanda jumped as he shouted but did as he asked. She sat her bottom down on the cold stone of the floor and shivered.

"What are you going to make me do?" she asked worried.

"Spread your legs," was all he said.

Amanda had never shown her body to someone else before and she felt humiliated but that only fuelled her arousal. She spread her legs wide and showed her sex to him. Terrence put a hand on his bulge and grunted with pleasure.

"You make me so horny you know that?" he started to pant as he felt the pre cum ooze out of him. "Will you be a good girl and do everything I say?" he asked as he groped his hand over himself and writhed in his seat.

Amanda nodded and felt herself grow swollen as she watched Terrence get more and more turned on. She couldn't think of a greater sight than watching him orgasm and she watched with wide eyes as she saw him touch himself.

"Spread your legs wider," he barked with no hint of tenderness. "I want to see everything,"

Amanda did as she was told and felt incredibly scared. On one hand she was here getting what she wanted but at the same time she never anticipated what it would really feel like to lose her virginity. And she could never have guessed what it would feel like to be so naked and vulnerable. The fear and excitement however made her aroused and as she traced her fingers down between her breasts she felt the deep need to plough them between her legs.

"Your tits, grip them hard!" Terrence said and Amanda held one of her enormous breasts in her hand.

She felt the hardness of her pink nipple between her thumb and forefinger and she noticed that they'd never felt to sensitive before. Lifting up her breasts she placed the nipple between her lips and licked it softly. It was enough to make Terrence feel he couldn't control his arousal any longer and he pulled his pants down. His penis sprung from his underwear and was so large the tip reached above his belly button. He started to massage the end with his fingers and leaned back into the feeling of pleasure. Amanda was shocked at the size of his manhood and wanted to crawl over and lick the entire length of it with a hungry tongue. She began to move and Terrence stopped her:

"Behave! You sit over there where I told you,"

And Amanda crawled back to her designated spot.

"Now touch yourself,"

Amanda knew that only the lightest of touches would bring her to climax as she felt her swollen clitoris. She moaned in deep pleasure as she slid two fingers around either side of it.

"Are you close?"

"Urgh…Yes. I'm gonna cum,"

"Don't! You're not allowed to unless I say so,"

"Oh no… I'm so close!" Amanda removed her hand so she didn't orgasm but it enraged the sheriff.

"What did I tell you? You touch yourself,"

And she did and it was the most exquisite torture. She was desperate to cum and each stroke of her fingers brought her close to doing so but of course she was not permitted to. She tried her best to control her feelings and think of things to distract herself. It worked for a while but she soon found herself losing control. This was especially because the sight of watching Terrence moving his hand up and down his penis was the most gorgeous thing she'd ever seen. She loved the way his hips moved up to meet his hand and the way his abs contracted as he gyrated but most of all she loved the look on his face; heated concentration mixed with ecstasy. She imagined herself climbing on top of his lap and lowering herself down onto him.

"Sheriff I can't do it anymore!" she cried, "I can't hold on!"

Terrence could see the desperation in her eyes and knew that she was as close to climax as he was.

"Very well. Come here," and he waved a finger in a hither to motion. "On your knees,"

She crawled over to him and sat between his legs like the faithful and obedient girl she wanted to be.

"Good girl! Now stick out your tongue,"

And she did. She tried to stick it out as far as it would go as she strained herself to please him.

"Now close your eyes,"

She clamped them shut quickly and waited for her next order.

Meanwhile Terrence moved forward with his penis still in his hand and placed the tip only centimetres away from her lips.

"Are you ready?"

She nodded, although she wasn't sure what she should be ready for. He teased her first and just placed it on her lips. She kissed it gently and wetted the tip. He rubbed it around her lips softly so she could get used to the size and feel and she eagerly wrapped her lips around it more and more and until the head was fully in her mouth. She struggled though and was sure she'd choke if she were to attempt anymore. Terrence groaned loudly as she sucked hard and he felt the dire need to grab the back of her head and thrust hard. He of course did not do this an instead lovingly swept back the hair from her face and held her head in his hands as though it were the most precious thing he'd ever seen.

"You're perfect Amanda," he whispered through his groans. "Can you go a little deeper?"

She leant forward a touch more and instantly gagged, reeling back in shock.

"It's ok, you don't have to do anything you don't want," the sheriff soothed.

Eventually Amanda opened her eyes and saw the full size of him in front of her, it was enormous and she couldn't stop herself from touching it. She reached out a hand and massaged it up and down the length but Terrence stopped her quickly.

"Oh God I'll just die if you keep doing that," he smirked. "I'm so close I can't stand it,"

"Me too," she said as she flicked out a tongue and teased him again.

"Are you ready?"

"More than ever,"

"Good, come here," he gestured for her to jump up on his lap which she did as quickly as she could. "Now carefully…. Go at your own pace,"

Amanda started to lower herself down onto his penis and was immediately flooded with the feeling of both pain and pleasure. She screamed and bit her hand.

"Am I your first?"

She nodded.

"I'm such a lucky man," Terrence looked up to her face to see her twisted expression of ecstasy.

She lowered herself down a bit further until the pain stopped and pleasure took its place and she found her own rhythm as she rode up and down the length. It was however so big that it made it impossible for her to supress an orgasm and she fell into his chest as she contracted onto him.

"Urgh…. Sorry!" Amanda knew she had disobeyed him but thankfully he couldn't control himself either.

"Oh fuck!" he cried and his thighs shuddered violently as he pumped inside her.

"Don't stop!" Amanda yelled. "I want more!"

And Terrence wasn't anywhere near satisfied yet either so he gripped her waist hard and bounced her up and down like a doll. This time he went deeper and deeper until her screams were so loud he was certain Tony could hear them upstairs. Amanda leaned into his neck and whispered:

"You can be even rougher if you like?"

And Terrence couldn't control himself. As he placed his bearish hands around her throat she reached her second orgasm shaking and squirming onto him. Seeing her pleasure was the best thing the sheriff could have imagined and a hundred times more arousing than it had been in his dreams. He thrust as hard as he could into her feeding off her wetness and heightened state of arousal and before long he also came for a second time. He held her body close to his as he felt himself ejaculate inside her. He kissed the space between her breasts as he regained his breath. She wrapped her arms around him tightly. Now that it was over Amanda wasn't sure whether she had dreamt the whole experience, it was so perfect and everything she wanted.

The couple sat for a long while gazing into each other's eyes as they recovered. Now that they had both been satisfied the reality of the situation had hit them. Amanda looked around and noticed the grimness of the cell for the first time but the sordid dirtiness of it all made her happy. She always thought there was some sort of faded glamor and hidden decadence to squalor.As if it the dirt manifested itself from some part of her squalid fantasies. She kissed him one last time and then jumped up to dress herself.

"Sheriff I think you ought to get back to work,"

"Haha that's it, wham bam thank you mam?" he joked but he knew too that their absence was suspicious. "Well missy you better hurry back to the house now and wait for me, this isn't over yet," a huge grin spread across his face.

"And what should I do when I get there?" she asked with her little pout and baby voice.

"You want orders?"

She nodded.

"Well I want you to hurry home and take yourselves upstairs to my bedroom. In the top drawer by my bed there'll be a spare set of handcuffs,"

Amanda's eyes widened with excitement.

"Then I want you to strip naked and lie on the bed making sure to leave the window open. I want you cold and bored when I get back so you'll be even more pleased to see me," Terrence laughed.

"Anything else?"

"Yes! I want you to cuff one arm to the bed and leave the other free. Your task for the rest of the day is to wait for me without ever touching yourself once," Terrence nodded triumphantly as he explained his cruel plan.

"But that's impossible! How long must I wait?"

"As long as I take, you don't complain you just do it. I may be home in an hour or I may be home at midnight. Do you think you're up to it?"

Amanda stood in silence for a long while as she thought about it.

"I don't know I mean….what do I get from it? What's my reward if I'm a good girl?"

"Haha… Good question… If I catch you touching yourself you will be severely punished. If you behave yourself on the other hand I'll make sure to spoil you like a princess and when I'm finished you'll have had so many orgasms the thought of another one would be torture," he grinned that cheeky smile of his again and Amanda melted.

"It's a deal! I can do it,"

"Well I don't think you can but prove me wrong. Now you hurry outta here now. I better get back to work," and he slapped her ass playfully and kissed her.

As he let Amanda leave the basement before him he watched her from behind as she ascended the stairs. *What a perfect girl*, he thought to himself. *She fulfils every fantasy.* He heard her make polite chat with Tony and then leave through the main entrance and it gave him enough time to compose himself before having to face his deputy who must have certainly heard them. He pushed the door open.

"Afternoon sheriff," Tony said meekly as he looked straight down to his desk to avoid looking at his boss.

"Did I miss anything?"

"Nothing," Tony still looked at his desk as if it was the most fascinating piece of furniture he'd ever seen. "Well I better patrol the town," he blurted out quickly.

"Yup…" Was all Terrence could say before he watched the deputy scurry out of the station.

CHAPTER 13

Amanda slammed the front door behind her as she entered the house. As she ran upstairs she worried about leaving Helen at Mrs Wheen's for so long but at the same time she knew she'd be having fun over there. She quickly dismissed the thought as she ran into Terrence's bedroom and flung open the top drawer. The handcuffs sat proudly in the drawer along with a hand gun and some bullets.

"If only I knew this was here months ago!" she lamented to herself as she felt the cold steel between her fingers.

She slipped a wrist through one of the holes and snapped it shut as tightly as she could. She felt a deep satisfaction from feeling that restraint and to her the tightness around her skin felt like a kiss. She pretended to wriggle free from the cuffs and enjoyed the stinging sensation on her wrist bone as she struggled to break free. She took it off and placed it back in the drawer. This was almost too much, there was no way she could fulfil her order without giving in. She sat on the side of the bed looking into the top drawer as she readied herself mentally for the task at hand. Looking at the clock she saw it was 4 which meant it wouldn't be too long until he was home unless…… he did one of his very few late nights at the station. Looking out the window she saw the sun begin to dip behind the trees and she knew it was only a matter of time before the temperature dropped. Regardless she opened the window and felt the cool breeze.

"I can do this," she whispered to herself as she began to undress.

Her nipples stood erect and hard as the cool wind hit them and she shivered slightly before lying on top of the bed. She happily clamped a cuff around one wrist and fastened the other end to the head board. Done. All she had to do was wait. But was it really that simple? Only seconds had passed and she felt fidgety already with a mixture of boredom and apprehension. She thought back to earlier and felt a mighty satisfaction at having lost her virginity to the man of her dreams. She remembered his taught, muscular arms as they held onto her both affectionately and possessively. Amanda so desperately wanted him to be here with her, to feel his big hands and hard body and look into those infinite eyes that looked at her like she was a god.

That feeling came back again, tingles and heat, and she sensed it would be impossible to keep her hand from wondering. The clock on the wall said quarter past 4, how could time have moved so slowly? Amanda felt as if she had been lying in wait for an eternity.

For a long while she passed the minutes by examining every single item in the room and trying to remember their places in her mind so that when she was to leave, she could close her eyes at will and be back in the sheriff's bed. She practised a few times and was both surprised and delighted to find that her memory was working brilliantly. Closing her eyes and imagining the room, she could see every vivid detail in her mind. The 23 floorboards that ran the length of the room, the 5 books on the shelf, the 7 shirts hanging loosely and the crack in the upper right corner of the wall in front her. Next she moved onto the smells and focused on the earthen, dryness that came from the room that was accentuated by the smell of a man; sweat and musk in the clothes and seed on the bedsheets. She breathed it in deeply so she'd never forget.

Next were her physical feelings like that of the cuff around her wrist and the pillows beneath her head. She moved from the top of her head to her feet taking in every single sensation of being there and she finished the game by pressing her toes hard into the wooden board at the end of the bed so she could cement the feelings in her mind. Now all she had to do when she was alone in her bed was to close her eyes and she could be transported straight back here with every authentic detail. She felt pleased with herself for creating such an efficient distraction but when she read the clock she saw it was barely 5. She huffed and wriggled in the bed.

The air in the room was starting to chill and out the window Amanda could see the sun had almost vanished to a miniscule glowing disk behind the trees. In a moment it would look as though it would atomize and dissipate into the earth as it disappeared. The darkness brought a fresh set of challenges as now she felt miserably cold and could see nothing in the room. Over time her eyes began to adjust but only enough to see rough outlines of the furniture.

Amanda began to lose all sense of time in the darkness and every minute seemed to last an hour as her mind began to play tricks on her. Shadows formed in the corners of the room and at the sides of her eyes. She knew that they were just figments of her imagination but that did nothing to stop the fear inside her as she constantly flitted her eyes around the room. She never did like the dark but right now, cuffed to the bed, she had no choice but to face her fears. The only other option would be to disobey her master and that was the last thing she wanted to do.

As the house cooled down in the night air each piece of wood and metal seemed to be contracting as the floorboards creaked and the pipes groaned. To Amanda it sounded like Terrence's boots and every creak brought hope that he was home but of course he wasn't. She thought about him for the thousandth time and felt her fingers creep down her thighs. Stopping herself she wriggled to try and shake away the feeling of arousal but the more she tried to distract herself the worse it became.

The cold was making her shiver uncontrollably as the wind blew in through the window. She looked out to the moon that was high in the sky and noticed that it was starting to illuminate parts of the bedroom. Finally she could see the clock again and it was nearly half past 10.

"Oh my God! Where is he?" Amanda worried that she might go insane.

But she knew that the keys to the cuffs were only inches away from the bed and the more she lay there feeling frustrated the more she kept looking over to them. They began to tempt her in the way that food tortures the hungry and a quick grab and turn of the key would put an end to her misery. She could be warm, comfortable and satisfied if she just gave in and let herself go. But she'd come this far already so there was no giving in. She didn't want to disappoint the sheriff. In fact more than anything she wanted to please him and show him that she was the good girl that he wanted. Having broken through the mental wall of weakness she steeled herself to see this through to the end.

She focussed on the ticking of the clock and looked out at the stars. Occasionally they would be obscured by the clouds but then the wind would blow them away into wisps and she could see them again. Her father was always good at finding the constellations and she remembered back to many happy nights out on the porch with her sisters as he would regale them with tales of the Big Dipper. Yet as she looked out now she couldn't find any of them and the thought upset her. It wasn't long until moonlight soothed her and sleep took her from her worries as she dozed off dreaming of home.

A loud bang snapped her from her dreams and she woke up with a jump as though she had fallen from a great height. It was the bedroom door closing as Terrence made sure to slam it hard.

"Wakeywakey little girl!" he said loudly with an authority in his voice that made Amanda's heart flutter. "Have you been a good girl?"

"Oh I have! I did everything you said,"

"You promise?"

Amanda nodded and made a little whimper.

"Because if I find out that you're lying you'll be in for a world of trouble,"

"I promise sheriff, I've done everything you asked of me. I didn't even touch myself I've just been laying here, I promise!" she pleaded.

Terrence lit a candle and stood for a moment looking at the beautiful spectacle in his bed. A quick glance into her desperate eyes showed him that she was telling the truth but he knew that she would do what he said. He was the sheriff after all. He placed the candle in a holder and put it by the bed. It made Amanda's eyes glow brilliantly like a cat's and it illuminated her perfect, large breasts that rose up into little cold and stiff peaks.

"Are you sure you didn't even touch these" he asked as he pulled gently at her nipples. "Because I wouldn't be able to control myself around them," he licked softly and cupped one in his mouth. He loved to feel the bumpiness of her areola on his tongue and the hardness between his lips.

"I didn't," Amanda said proudly. "Not even once!"

"Good girl!" grunted Terrence as he hungrily sucked on her.

Amanda eased back into the feeling of pleasure and felt so proud of herself for not giving in. She was finally being rewarded. Terrence lay on top of her and cradled her caringly in his arms. Kissing her softly he stroked her hair and Amanda had never felt so secure and loved in all her life. He traced his fingers down her body and stopped just below her navel kissing her softly all the way down.

He moved down and placed himself between her legs in a way that signalled to Amanda that he would be there for some time. Just feeling his body there, only inches away from her sex, made her turned on in a way that was indescribable. Terrence brushed his lips so softly up the inside of her thigh and the feeling of his rough stubble was exquisite against her soft skin. He began to nuzzle in at her inner thigh and kiss her with soft strokes of his tongue. He was only a few centimetres away from her clitoris and she felt the compulsive need to wriggle wildly so that he could kiss her there. But of course he didn't and he clamped his hands around her pelvis and pushed her into the bed.

"Behave! You'll get your reward properly if you don't play up," the sheriff scalded her.

Amanda immediately stayed as stiff as a board in worry of displeasing him and tried to control her feelings as he teased her for the longest time. After several minutes she finally felt that gorgeous, rough stubble start to creep over and graze the side of her pussy lips. *Urgh, so close*, she thought to herself and desperately tried to stay still but she knew that even the slightest sensation on her clitoris would made her writhe in ecstasy.

He flicked his tongue out tentatively and lightly brushed her clitoris. She moaned loudly and flung back her head into the pillow. The dramatic arch of her back accentuated her perfect breasts and Terrence couldn't help himself from reaching up and running his hands down the length of her body.

He licked her a little harder this time and the scream Amanda let out was the most erotic thing Terrence had ever heard. He felt his hardness in his pants and he pushed it against the bed to feel some pressure. Wanting to give her the best time of her life her cupped his lips around her but didn't suck yet, but rather he teased her a little while longer with just his hot breath lingering on her. She began to squirm and drive her hips upward to grind herself against his face but yet again he gripped her hips hard and pushed her back down.

So very gently he began to suck on her clitoris as if it were the juiciest fruit, with his tongue softly lapping at her and his lips never leaving her skin. He felt the lashings of wetness that flowed from her and he pushed in a finger slowly to touch her g spot. She instantly began to shake and he knew that to tease her any longer would be the sweetest but most cruel torture. He relented and began to push hard inside her over and over and in one quick movement he sucked as hard and as quickly as he could.

Amanda felt as though her orgasm was ripping through her body in a torrent of pleasure as she shuddered and screamed. Her free hand was pulling at Terrence's hair and for a moment she worried that she was hurting him but at the same time she felt like control had left her body. She rose up her pelvis one last time as the last ounce of orgasmic pleasure began to leave.

For a moment only silence filled the room with infrequent punctuations of heavy breathing. Amanda looked to the ceiling and felt her vision returning to normal as though she were waking from the most vivid dream. Her immediate reaction was to feel the need to cuddle and sleep as the pleasure had physically exhausted her. But as her eyelids grew heavy she felt Terrence climb on top of her and stroke her face.

"Come on sleeping beauty, we're not finished yet," he smiled as he unzipped his pants. "You know what would be fun?" the most mischievous grin twitched his lips as he took his work handcuffs from his belt. "Let's get that other hand all tethered up here," and he reached up and cuffed Amanda's free arm to the headboard. "All done!" he looked down at his handy work and felt satisfied.

Meanwhile Amanda loved the feeling of being even more restrained and she eased back into the "punishment" with a feeling of security. Terrence grew harder as he saw the pleasure in Amanda's eyes and he pulled himself out if his pants eagerly. He stroked himself up and down and groaned.

"I could never get enough of you," he stroked harder and thrust his hips forward quickly to meet his hand.

He couldn't hold it much longer though and so he took hold of Amanda's hips and held them up so he could get a better grip and reach deeper into her. He held himself close to her for a moment, brushing his tip gently around her petals. She was wet and swollen and the more

Terrence teased her the more he thought about how good it would feel to be inside of her. He pushed the head in slightlyand felt the pleasure envelope the most sensitive part of his body.

"Urrrrghhhhhhh…..fuck. I need you so much," and then he thrust hard.

Amanda screamed as that sense of fullness flooded her and blood rushed between her legs. She felt as though all her body's nerve endings lay in one place and she had never felt so sensitive. Terrence placed a thumb on her clitoris as he pushed in deep to hit her g spot. She immediately climaxed and shuddered, screaming as she twisted her body and then she did something she had never done before. She squirted onto him just like he planned and he came hard as he felt her contract around his swollen penis.

Climaxing together they fell into each other panting. Terrence lay face down on her chest and tried to regain his breath as he continued to groan.

"Oh my God…..oh my God….. I've never had it like that before….." the sheriff was lost for words and couldn't articulate how intense the feeling had been. He kissed her gently and held onto her. "You're the best Amanda, that's all you need to know."

She beamed with satisfaction and pride as Terrence un-cuffed her and laughed.

"You're finally free!"

And Amanda moved her arms to get rid of the numbness. She hadn't realized quite how much pain she had been in but she'd do it all over again to feel that sweet sense of security and possession that Terrence gave her. She yawned and felt her satisfied body slip into slumber but she stopped herself falling asleep in case it would displease the sheriff.

"It's ok little girl. You deserve your sleep," he said as he stood up to close the window. "You know I was kinda joking about this part. Never thought you'd do it," he laughed as he slammed it shut. "You were a very good girl though for doing it," he lay down beside her and pulled up the bedsheet to his waist.

Amanda watched the moonlight bounce off the sweat on his chest and looked at how statuesque and powerful his body was. He rose up an arm and gestured for her to cuddle in.

"Come here beautiful. It's been too long since I've had a gorgeous woman in my bed," he kissed the top of her head.

She fell asleep smiling as she lay in the bearish arms of the sheriff.

CHAPTER 14

Amanda dreamed of riding a white horse through a field of wheat. She had heard a mysterious noise that had taken her away from the house and it worried her. A baby's cry perhaps or maybe it was an injured animal. She didn't know but she felt compelled to follow the sound until she could rescue it. In her dream her hair flowed below her waist and as she looked down she noticed that she was naked. But she also noticed that she felt no shame.

As she rode through the field she saw that the shafts of wheat began to float away and join the sky with each piece becoming a hazy mist. Soon the sky above and all around her was swirling with tiny clouds and she felt dreadfully lost. But that was until the noise she was following became louder and louder the more the wheat flew away.

Soon enough it had all disappeared and her horse stood bare in a barren field not unlike a tundra. She looked down and saw a bundle of fabric on the ground and thinking it was a baby she immediately leapt from her horse. Picking it up carefully, she opened the fragile package and as she pulled back the cloth a little face revealed itself. Amanda couldn't mistake those enormous watery, blue eyes and inquisitive expression far beyond its years.

"Helen?" she whispered and kissed the tiny forehead.

BANG! The sound of the bedroom door slamming shut jolted her from her sleep and she sat bolt upright in bed. She could hear Terrence's voice somewhere in the house and she realized she had slept in late. The door was swinging in the breeze as a draught travelled from somewhere in the house.

"Shit! Helen!" she jumped out of bed and quickly dressed herself before running downstairs.

"Well look who decided to get up?" Terrence joked as he placed a bowl of oats down for Helen's breakfast.

"Hi sweety!" she gave the little girl a big hug. "I'm so sorry I couldn't make it back over to Mrs Wheen's last night,"

"Oh I don't care," came the arrogant little reply that startled the governess. "I had loads of fun and she baked me cookies and told me stories," Helen smiled and shovelled a spoonful of porridge in her mouth before grimacing. "This is gross though,"

Terrence couldn't help but laugh because hearing his daughter sound so confident was music to his ears. He would have to work on her manners though.

"Hey well you can make your own breakfast next time,"

"I want Amanda to do it. She always makes the best!" Helen protested and huffed.

"I can do that my little pumpkin," smiled the governess as she set to work on pleasing the little girl.

Terrence smirked at the two girls and laughed.

"Well I'll leave you little princesses to it!" and without a thought he kissed Amanda goodbye and left with a spring in his step.

Helen of course noticed and Amanda blushed.

"I always knew my daddy liked you," Helen smiled the cheekiest smile that was only reserved for when she was naughty. Her little dimples always lit up Amanda's day.

~

And so the great romance began and Amanda's days were filled with great happiness and fulfilment. This of course was a great improvement on the perpetual sense of lustful longing and constant day dreaming that often filled her days. Each morning she would now wake up feeling alive and very much loved in the arms of Terrence who had now shed his almost mythical status of "the sheriff", a statuesque demi god in which to spend every day mentally worshipping, and was now her lover.

The birds were chirping outside as dawn glowed hopeful embers over the Wyoming landscape. It wasn't quite morning but Amanda was grateful to have woken up earlier than usual and could thus appreciate the loving embrace a little while longer. Soon enough Helen's little feet would come slapping down the hall before she'd cheekily enter the room and jump on the bed in a fit of giggles and cuddles. It was a newly formed habit that brought extraordinary joy to the governess. To feel like a family unit as the three of them dressed together each morning before making their way downstairs to begin the mundane activities of breakfast. Well, mundane to most, but it was a gorgeous feeling for Amanda who relished the opportunity to play mother.

It was Sunday morning and as the previous night's sky had predicted the day had erupted with a colourful celestial dawn. Day broke through the window and illuminated the bed in which the happy couple lay. Amanda draped her fingers off the end of the bed and the sun tickled off her skin. She wound her fingers around the beam of light that fell through the glass like a ray from the heavens and she felt its warmth. It did however trail off far behind her and as she turned to see where it ended she saw that it was bouncing off the corner of something that appeared to be making a miserly attempt at hiding itself.

Amanda rose quietly and made a very conscious effort to not make the bed springs creak as she stood up. It was of course a futile effort because the bed was as old as she was and was therefore a rickety catastrophe. She mentally vowed to mention it to Terrence once he awoke. But taking her attention back to the mysterious glimmer she saw that the sun was bouncing of the corner of something that was hiding behind the corner of something else; a frame behind another frame. She looked at the framed passage of the bible that was always placed by Terrence's bed. A piece of furnishing that often made Amanda feel terribly awkward as they made love beside it. But of course it gave her that little twinkle of naughty mischief that she enjoyed so much. She wondered what God would think of their exploits. A wry smile twitched her lips as she picked up the frame but quickly vanished when she saw what lay behind it.

Evangeline… Her face hidden behind the Bible passage as if God could protect her from the sins Terrence was committing in front of her. Amanda gasped and placed it back quickly. She saw the glass was still broken but her photo as always was as intact and beautiful as ever. She felt a tremendous guilt as she climbed back into bed and placed an arm around the beautiful man beside her. She was a usurper… or so she felt; scarlet woman who had intruded on a family and assumed the place of mother. As she saw the fluttering eyelids of Terrence as he woke from a dream she wondered why he felt the need to hide Evangeline's image. But she had no intention of asking him.

~

"See you later my sweetheart," Terrence kissed Amanda goodbye as he left for the station. "And of course I'll see you later as well," he kissed his daughter and gave her a little wave that made her giggle and bounce.

"I love it when it's just us too!" the little girl beamed as she gripped hold of her governess' hand.

"Me too!" Amanda touched Helen's hair and felt the silkiness between her fingers. As always she had ensured that the little girl was immaculately groomed with the finest things her father could buy.

"So what are we doing today? Are you going to teach me about the stars like you said you would?"

Amanda felt a pang of sadness as she remembered her father. She should really go back and visit soon. But how could she while she was continuing this sordid affair? Her mother would be appalled! But if Terrence were to marry her… Things would be different. Amanda felt herself grow giddy as the thought of marriage struck her for the first time. Her mind drifted off into a candy coated fantasy but was quickly pulled back as the little girl beside her yanked at her fingers.

"Well… are you?"

"Oh! The stars! I'm afraid not. Maybe another time," she lied and closed the front door.

Helen huffed and shuffled her feet, pretending to kick angrily at the floorboards, a rather hilarious and adorable form of protest that her governess had grown used to.

"Don't do that, you'll scuff the floor," she laughed. "Say! How about we go on a picnic?" Amanda offered to placate the little girl's grumpiness.

Helen instantly looked up with those big eyes and twinkled. "A picnic? Yey!!!" and she ran head first into Amanda's tummy as she threw her arms around her.

"Excellent! That way I can teach you about the flowers and the animals,"

"I love animals!"

"I know you do! And if you hurry up and change into your boots and get your coat then we can get there in time for you to meet the new subjects of your royal court,"

Helen stood back in a mixture of excitement and curiosity.

"Eh?" was all the little girl could say as she looked up to her governess.

"That's right! Didn't you know that bunnies make the perfect ladies in waiting for little princesses?" Amanda said as though that was that most normal thing ever uttered.

Helen meanwhile looked ecstatic and wavered for only a second before she ran up the stairs screaming in a hurry to get ready.

"Be careful pumpkin! Don't run or you'll trip!" Amanda shouted up the stairs but it was too late. She could already hear little footsteps bounding quickly down the hall above her.

~

"These are my favourite," said Helen as she smelt the sweet smell of pink roses. "They're the prettiest ones here,"

"But they're not as pretty as you my pumpkin" and the governess bopped her on the nose.

"Which ones are your favorites?" the little girl asked.

"Hmmm….." Amanda thought for a minute as she looked around the meadow. "I think these ones are," she brushed her hands across an enormous bush of daylilies. "They remind me of sunshine and warm flames trying to escape from a fireplace.

"Those ones remind me of my mom's hair," Helen said flatly but looked regretful the moment Amanda spun round in shock.

"Your mother's hair?" Amanda tried to put organize her thoughts so that she could understand what the girl was saying but she just couldn't. "What do you mean?"

"My first mommy, Evangeline, she had hair that color of orange. Like flames of desire I heard my daddy once say to his deputy. I don't know what that means though but I do know that it was pretty,"

Amanda reeled back. She couldn't believe what she was hearing. Her mother had died in childbirth and the only photograph of her in the house was in black and white. For a moment she pondered the idea that the girl had seen her ghost and she was terrified that the first woman of the house would be haunting the sheriff's home out of anger and betrayal. But she quickly dismissed that thought as silly. Gathering herself and kneeling down on the ground before the little girl who had no idea of the impact of her words, she spoke softly:

"Pumpkin… Where have you seen your mommy's hair?"

"In the box," was all she said before she began to nervously pick at the rose petals in her hand.

"And what box would that be?"

"You know… the one in the attic,"

Amanda was as aware of the box as she was of the existence of an attic. Although she assumed at times that the vast expanse of the room would contain some free space the thought of things being contained in its vicinity had eluded her.

"You go up to the attic a lot?" she asked Helen as she gulped back a terrible sense of anxiety.

"Not really," the girl shook her head coyly. "Just when you're out running errands, daddy and I are home,"

The revelation hit Amanda like a bolt of lightning. Not only was Terrence hiding away the existence of the attic but was also waiting until she left the house to go there. What on earth could he be hiding? She felt betrayed by him or in some ways betrayed by his past as she discovered it had been lingering above her head the entire time she had been in the house.

She leaned into Helen and kissed her cheek. The smell of roses was overwhelming as she took the fallen petals from between the girl's fingers.

"Say pumpkin, how do you fancy a little trip to Mrs Wheen's?" Amanda held onto her hands and spoke sternly as she tried her best to masquerade her hurt as playfulness. "I do believe she might bake you some of her pecan cookies," she smiled as falsely as was possible making sure the act was not to slip.

Helen nodded and giggled.

"I love Mrs Wheen!"

"I know you do kitten,"

CHAPTER 15

The door to the attic was almost invisible at first but as she looked up to the ceiling of Helen's bedroom she could see the faint outline of a little square. It looked too small to be an entrance to something though but on closer inspection Amanda thought she could fit through her head and shoulders.

She climbed up onto Helen's sideboard and momentarily felt guilty for stepping her great big, adult boots onto such a delicate and feminine surface. But that was until she looked down and saw marks that indicated adult boots had stepped on this surface many times already. She poked her finger into the square and it shifted easily. This little section of the ceiling was made of a light and mobile material and Amanda felt no difficulty in pushing it up and moving it to the side.

The governess was instantly hit by the smell of antiquity. The musty and mouldy air tickled at her face and was so strong she could taste it. She chewed it around her mouth and grimaced. Clutching a handkerchief to her face she reached up as high as she could and felt the inside of the square opening. Brushing against her fingers was the sharp and wooden corner of a set of stairs and as she pulled gently they fell down loosely. All Amanda had to do then was climb right up.

A cobweb caught her cheek as he reached the top of the steps. For a moment she thought it was the gentle hand of a mysterious figure. She spun round terrified but instantly saw that nothing was keeping her company except for the occasional spider that thread its way through the floorboards. To Amanda there didn't seem to be anything of any interest hidden up above the house except for the existence of the space itself.

She tread carefully, terrified that a loose floorboard would send her tumbling. Amanda wasn't quite sure what was worse; the falling through the floor and getting hurt or falling and being discovered by an angry sheriff who would have caught her snooping. She decided that both were just terrible and so she decided to err on the side of caution and only walk on the boards where she could see were most used. It was easy to tell after all because these were the ones with the least dust. They followed a clear path to the back of the attic and it led her to an area which she assumed to be the space above porch. A tiny porthole window stood before her like a watchful eye and her covert behaviour suddenly felt rather shameful. Holding her face to the glass she couldn't see a thing. It had grown dirty and black in its old age, a reason, she surmised, as to why she hadn't noticed it from the outside before.

There wasn't much to look at here except for the window and she wondered what could possibly make this the most popular spot in the attic. But as she turned to walk away she felt a floorboard creak beneath her and she instinctively looked down for signs of danger. Except there were none but there was however something else. Amanda noticed that her foot had caught a rebellious floorboard which had sprung from its holding place. Bending down to take a closer look she saw that a large gap sat beneath the board. *Curious*, she thought to herself as she knelt down. The board came away easily from the rest of the flooring and as Amanda looked down she saw there was a sizeable compartment beneath her. She was however too timid of grime and spiders to arbitrarily dip her hand in. Searching about for a candle she quickly saw found atop an old dresser next to some matches that lay discarded in a soggy box. To her surprise she manged to spark one and lighting the candle she could now see about the attic more clearly.

Kneeling down once more at the hole in the floor she carefully lowered the candle down. For being in such a hidden and musty part of the house Amanda was shocked and someone concerned to see that it was immaculate and not dusty at all. *Someone must take good care of this little nook*, she thought as she bent her head down. *I wonder why that is*. But there it was… the reason. It was a mahogany trunk the size of a small hat box and as Amanda reached a hand down to touch it she could feel its smooth and conditioned wood. Terrence must have been taking good care of this special possession although in over a year at living in the house she had never seen him hold it. But then again she had never been in the attic. It appeared the Evan's family was bearing more secrets than she first realized.

The trunk was difficult to lift out despite its small size. It was heavy and Amanda guessed that it was filled with valuable trinkets. She was right too for when she opened it images, gems and metals flashed before her eyes. Yet while these were most definitely treasure they were not of the priceless kind. They were mementos of the heart and contained precious memories of a life long gone.

There were three photographs. Large depictions printed on rough card that felt sturdy between Amanda's fingers despite the fact that she noticed they had been handled a thousand times already. One was of a little girl who could have been Helen if it weren't for two things; the background showed a household that was much older than this house and the little girl's hair was not pale blonde. Yet those enormous eyes beckoned for her love as she looked into them.

The second photograph was taken outside in a stable and for all the governess could have guessed it could have been the stable of this very house. A striking woman stood in front of a young Betsy who looked regal and radiant with a mane decorated with flowers. The woman however was a hundred times more striking. A thousand times even more so as her hip length hair cascaded down the sides of a laced up blouse. Those eyes were unforgettable and to Amanda it now seemed obvious that Helen had very much inherited her mother's looks. She would never be able to play with the little girl in the same way again. Evangeline's face was a refined yet strong one and at first glance it was obvious how Terrence could have fallen in love with such a character.

Amanda felt a lump rise in her throat and no amount of swallowing would make it go away. She was jealous and that made her feel wretched. *Jealous of a dead woman, how could I be?* And there was in fact no need to be because she now had Evangeline's position didn't she? Except that was the problem. She thought that no matter how much Terrence made love to her his heart would always be with Evangeline.

A deep dread set into her heart as she looked at the last photograph. It was of a couple on their wedding day. young and vibrant with eyes that shone with ambition and love. She couldn't look anymore and so placed the three photographs face down on the floor.

"What the hell was Helen talking about? Hair? Orange hair?" she felt bewildered as she rummaged through the box some more.

Then her finger caught something sharp and she pulled away hurt. A drop of blood fell from her skin and onto her dress. She had pricked herself rather carelessly on a pin of sorts. She looked closer to see it was the fastening on a brooch which, to Amanda at least, looked worn out and beyond repair. Bezels with missing gems sat in metal that was tarnished with years of neglect. It was not massively pleasing to the governess' eyes but what lay beneath it grabbed her attention.

It was the brightest object in the trunk and shone like sunshine through the aged items. Bright auburn hair, sat within a glass receptacle not unlike a pocket watch. *A memento mori*, Amanda thought, a tangible memory of the dead. A tiny handwritten note also sat within the glass and she squinted to read it.

Locket of hair taken at the bed of Evangeline Evans.

April 28th, 1905.

That was Helen's birthday! And Amanda's heart sank as she realized what that meant. She placed the item back in the box and tumbled the photographs back on top and prayed Terrence wouldn't notice the items were touched. The trunk was then placed back as best as she remembered and the floorboard slid into place. She hurried to the steps and looked back quickly to ensure she hadn't made any obvious footprints in the dust. Quickly sliding through the square hole and shimmying down the steps, she shut the attic opening and jumped down from the dresser. Paying close attention to clear up any mess she made she then went to Mrs Wheen's house as if nothing ever happened.

CHAPTER 16

"You're acting real strange tonight you know that?" Terrence said as he pointed a fork with a potato skewered on the end at her.

"Strange?" she feigned curiosity.

"Yeah like… quiet and stuff,"

"Weird… Sorry I don't mean to be. Just a little tired is all,"

Terrence shrugged and put the potato in his mouth. He nodded in approval.

"Great dinner as always," he said cheerfully before leaning over and kissing the governess on the cheek.

"Thank you," she blushed happily.

The truth was that Terrence had arrived home not two minutes after Amanda had climbed out of the attic. Her heart had been in her mouth ever since with a mixture of nervousness and anger. He was keeping secrets from her! But at least now she knew. She wasn't sure however whether she should let it go and assume it was a private ritual of grieving or ask him what he was playing at. She guessed the former… The poor man was entitled to his memories after all. Still though, only hours later she sat at the dinner table with quite possibly the worst poker face. She never was good at hiding secrets and she'd have to tell him eventually that she'd been up in the attic. Just not today.

Meanwhile Terrence was perturbed. He'd been in law enforcement for fifteen years and knew a liar when he saw one. *What was she hiding?* He chewed on his dinner thoughtfully as he looked at the skittish girl across the table. Helen thought, oblivious to the entire scene, was merrily kicking her feet under the table and humming to herself joyfully. Her blonde hair bounced from side to side as she enjoyed her dinner but as adorable as she was she was annoying the sheriff. He'd had a long day and needed time to think.

"Hey Helen? Sweety? How about you head on up to bed when you've finished eating and I'll read you one of your favorite stories eh?"

"Really?" she quickly got excited. "But you hardly ever read to me anymore!"

"I know sweety and I'm real sorry about that but it'll be just like the old days won't it,"

Helen nodded enthusiastically and her curls flopped everywhere. She shovelled in the last few mouthfuls of food and ran upstairs.

"It's a bit early isn't it?" Amanda asked with suspicion.

"It's never too early to spend time with my daughter," was all he said before he also disappeared and left Amanda alone with a table of dirty dishes.

The truth was that he just wanted away from Amanda for a few hours. She was lying about something he was sure of it. Maybe Helen knew more than he ever could, those two were thick as thieves.

He waited until Helen was in her favourite pyjamas and was all comfortable and tucked in before picking out a book from the living room and heading upstairs.

"Ready princess?" he asked as he opened the door to see a beaming little angel amongst all the pink and frills.

"Ready!"

But before Terrence could sit down he noticed something. It was a policeman's hunch more than anything, a feeling that things were not as they seemed. He looked about and everything looked pretty normal. He looked closer and his own mind started to doubt him. Was everything in its place? Something looked different, what was it? The dresser? He looked at all the girly sundries placed upon it and at first glance all seemed normal except for one doll. It lay on its side and to anyone else it wouldn't mean a thing. Except that Helen's things were always impeccably looked after and usually Amanda would make sure that nothing would be placed so untidily.

A thought struck him hard and he felt it in his gut. *The attic! Shit, the attic!* He craned his neck and glanced to the ceiling in a panic. The square, although in its place wasn't quite where it should be. A gap about an inch thick showed that the door had been opened recently and placed back in a hurry. So she was hiding something.

He sat on the edge of Helen's bed and flipped open the book as if nothing was wrong.

"Once upon a time there was a prince who wanted to marry a princess; but she would have to be a real princess. He travelled all over the world to find one, but nowhere could he get what he wanted." He began to read slowly and immediately Helen smiled and her dimples took away his worries.

~

Amanda knew her time was up. Terrence wasn't stupid he'd guessed already. She paced the length of the kitchen over and over and when she couldn't contain her nerves any longer she'd clean something just to expel some energy.

"Oh no!" she placed her head in her hands. "I should have just minded my own business," she whispered to herself praying that her words would somehow make her travel back in time. She'd ignore what Helen said in the meadow, she wouldn't ask any questions and she wouldn't be so possessive and jealous. Who cared if Terrence had his own things in the attic? It was none of her business was it? But why the secrecy?

"I'm just a governess? I should never have got involved in this silliness?" she sat at the table and tried to stifle the tears but it was impossible.

More than anything she feared that Terrence would hate her and send her packing. She'd have no choice but to return home jobless and heartbroken. She couldn't bear the thought of losing Terrence.

The minutes passed slowly in the darkness of the kitchen. Amanda knew it was only a matter of time until she'd hear those boots coming down the stairs angrily. He must have noticed the already and her mind raced as she cast her mind back to earlier. She was certain that she'd closed the attic door properly. She was also sure that everything on the dresser was tidied up. But then again she was in a hurry and could have forgotten to double check. Butterflies were tight in her stomach and she sipped at a glass of water to rid of herself of a dry mouth.

Soon enough what she feared came true. Those heavy steps came nearer and Amanda felt like a little girl that was in trouble with her father. Terrence stepped into the kitchen in a rage.

"Why were you up there?" he spoke quietly so as not to wake Helen but his teeth were clenched angrily. "Tell me! Why were you up there?"

"I….I don't know. Helen just…"

"Helen what?? Eh?"

There was no use trying to evade him and so she came clean.

"Helen had mentioned a box in the attic and I was curious…" it was all she could say and she felt pathetic.

"Why didn't you just ask me? I would have just taken you up there myself? Don't lie to me again! I know you're up to something! The photo of Evangeline? Your snooping in the attic? And your mysterious errands you've run when you've sent Helen to Mrs Wheen's?"

The governess opened her mouth in shock.

"That's right! Helen just told me! You made my daughter part of this now too. You're so god damn selfish!"

Terrence was seething but at the same time wasn't having any measure of fun taking part in this drama. He lit a cigarette and looked into Amanda's eyes. She looked utterly petrified of him and he softened up for a moment feeling guilty.

"Look I'm not really that angry it's just that I hate being lied to. I'm a policeman remember? Don't think you can get away with this nonsense under my roof," he pointed the cigarette at her.

"I'm so sorry! Just so sorry!!! I… I can't even explain it. I just want to be with you so badly and well… I LOVE YOU so much. It's made me act in the craziest ways and do things I normally wouldn't. Just so that I could have the chance to be with you. Won't you please forgive me?"

The sheriff relented and slumped in a chair.

"You women are a funny bunch. Always doin' weird things for love, I guess you're excused. For now… But anymore funny business and you're outta here!" he tried to make the threat as genuine as possible but he knew deep down that he could never be without Amanda.

"That's it? You're not mad anymore?" Amanda was sceptical and couldn't imagine that she was off the hook so easily.

"That's it… Well maybe. Go to bed,"

"Hmmm?"

"You heard me women go to bed immediately," it was a stern order.

Amanda quickly jumped up and scurried to the stairs. She hesitated for a moment and turned around to see the sheriff looking at her from the kitchen. He didn't say a word but rather raised a finger and pointed it to the ceiling in a somewhat menacing way. She got the hint and ran upstairs.

CHAPTER 17

The bedroom was cold when the governess entered and she slammed the window shut as she shivered. The nights were getting longer now and usually it was a time of great misery to Amanda. She hated how the days got sucked into darkness as the year progressed but something about this year was different. Terrence obviously was a great comfort and now as the night engulfed the house she could relax in the candle light knowing that he was beside her. The thought warmed her as she changed into her nightgown and sat obediently on the edge of the bed.

Her nerves were electric inside of her and she worried about what Terrence was thinking. Would he punish her? Or would he give her the silent treatment? She hoped if she guessed right that all her dreams would come true.

The door opened slowly with a creak and at first all Amanda could see was the haze of smoke drifting up from the cigarette that hung from Terrence's mouth. His stature seemed enormous as it lingered in the doorway. For a moment Amanda actually felt a little frightened of him but as he stepped into the candle light his cheeky smile dissolved her worries.

"So you think you can get away with anything in this house eh?" he joked and walked over to her.

"Oh no sheriff! Not at all,"

Terrence knelt down in front of her and pushed her legs apart. He slid her nightgown up her thighs with his rough hands and was pleased to see that she wore nothing underneath.

"Good governess," he smiled and leaned forward.

For the most heavenly of seconds the sheriff sucked hard on her and Amanda lay back in ecstasy. She groaned loudly and writhed her hips up to meet his mouth. She wanted him harder and faster but just as she thought she was close to orgasm he pulled away. He rather politely rolled her nightgown back down and walked away.

"No. You don't get what you want today. You've been bad!" he said as he unbuckled his belt.

The glint off the metal buckle sparkled in Amanda's eyes and Terrence saw her excitement.

"Oh you like the look of this?" he pulled it off him and wrapped the buckled end around his hand before whipping the soft leather against the wooden floor.

It made a soft whooshing sound and then a crack as it hit the floor and just like in the corn field Amanda grew wet and excited. She wanted to feel the suppleness of the belt as it hit her hard. She imagined what it would feel like against the skin of her buttocks and she crawled her fingers down to touch herself. Terrence however was not happy.

"No!" he said loudly and strictly as he slapped her hand away. "You do as I say!"

She shrunk back in surprise but was secretly thrilled at his bossiness.

"Are you going to punish me sheriff? Are you going to do bad things to me?"

"Well that depends," he said thoughtfully and stroked his chin playfully as though he was in a deep pensive state. "I mean… Do you really want to be corrected? Do you really want to learn how to be a good girl? Or are you a rebel? A bad seed?"

"I want to be a good girl sheriff!"

"Good… That's what I wanted to hear. Well then you'll have to do as I say and relinquish yourself to me, your body and your mind. You have to promise that you'll lose control of yourself as I command every single inch of you,"

"I couldn't want anything more," she gasped and looked up lovingly into his eyes.

Terrence knelt back down beside her and looked into the beauty of her perfect face. *How could such a perfect creature be his?* He wondered. The candle light flared off her eyes giving her a cheeky glint as she smiled.

"Please correct me," she said in a raspy and eager voice before he moved forward and kissed her.

He held her face was tight in his hand as if he wanted to possess her. She moved her fingers out to touch his chest, to wrap herself around him but he pushed her away.

"You move when I say you move," he feigned anger. "Now let's get down to business,"

Amanda's heart thumped with excitement. But at first she wasn't sure what he was doing as he crawled under the bed. She could hear some mysterious and heavy noises that only revealed themselves once he slid out a heavy oak trunk. It was small in size but large in significance for when he opened it her eyes grew wide.

"The shackles…" she said in awe as though he had just showed her a hidden antiquarian treasure.

Terrence however looked up at her suspiciously.

"What do you mean THE shackles," he asked a little perplexed.

Amanda cursed herself for being so stupid. In her heightened state of arousal she had forgotten that Terrence didn't know she was in the cornfield on the day he beat Colt. The day she saw those shackles for the first time and felt the joy of watching the sheriff in a place of pure domination.

"I just mean… you know…" she stuttered. "You know like… just the shackles," it was a pathetic attempt at hiding her secret but she was pleased when he said nothing more.

He decided to ignore her stumbling words as another one of her idiosyncrasies and so carried on with his plan. Lifting the shackles out of their box they made a loud clanking sound as they hit the floor. They were heavier than Amanda could have imagined.

"Take that thing off," Terrence nodded to the nightgown.

She instantly ripped it off her body with little concern for its condition. She would have set fire to it if he'd asked. For a moment she dithered anxiously, wondering what Terrence would tell her to do next. She watched him untangle the chains before dropping them to the bed. They were so heavy they made the mattress sag in the middle.

"Now climb on the bed,"

Terrence, in the most methodical fashion, began to unravel it all with great pleasure. He secured Amanda's two feet to the end of the bed and then her hands to the top. He also gracefully created some beautiful knots in the chains and crossed them over her body. The final result was a spectacular image of submission, beautiful in its intricacy. Amanda was very much under his control and she loved the feeling.

The cold of the steel against her skin was a mix of pain and comfort. The weight of the chains felt, to Amanda at least, like a giant hug. She had never felt so secure as she lay tethered to the bed. For a long while Terrence walked around the bed from side to side in order to survey his handy work. He was pleased with himself at first but the more he inspected it the more he felt that he should tweak at the chains; little bit here and a little bit there until he was quite satisfied.

"Aren't you going to undress for me sheriff?" Amanda spoke out of turn, an act that could receive severe penalties but she genuinely wanted to know.

"Don't ask questions," barked Terrence who walked up the bed, running his hands over the chains and enjoying feeling every bump of metal beneath his skin.

More than anything Amanda was begging in her mind for him to touch her. She was desperate to know what his plan was and hoped that it wasn't for him to leave her alone, trussed up in the bedroom in the dark. And so she was very grateful when he sat down beside her and gazed at her body.

"You are so beautiful," he said as he stroked the side of her face.

Her nipples immediately stood erect at his touch and Terrence noticed. He brushed a fingertip over the top of one and felt its hardness. He then pinched it lightly and watched it grow even pinker.

"Do you like that?" he asked as leaned in closer.

Amanda nodded.

"How about a little harder?"

She nodded again.

This time he gripped it hard between his thumb and forefinger and squeezed. It brought a little shock of pain to Amanda who instantly winced and made a little whimper. The pain however made her wet and as he pulled his hand away, leaving her stinging, she exhaled deeply as she relaxed into the feeling.

"You like it when it hurts?"

"Uhuh…"

"And why's that sweetheart?"

Amanda tried to think of a reason but couldn't.

"I don't know….it just feels good," she tried to explain.

"I think so too," Terrence grinned. "How about a little harder again?"

"Yes please!"

And he gripped her nipple again, this time making the conscious effort to really squeeze and twist at her skin. Amanda screamed loudly and arched her back. It felt like a deep heat was rushing through her breast but the sensation brought her intense joy and she panted as the pain subsided.

"Let's see if you really did like it?" Terrence said with a peculiar look on his face.

He brushed his hand over her thighs and then pushed his fingers between her legs. He felt that she was wet and ready and he pulled his hand away, feeling the moisture still on his fingers.

"Looks like you really did!" he ran his fingers over his lips just to taste her.

It was a sight that greatly excited Amanda and she begged with her eyes for him to touch her again.

"You want more?"

She nodded.

"Very well,"

Terrence pushed his hand back and felt her clitoris that was slick and slippery beneath his fingers. She was also incredibly hot and swollen and he knew that she was at her most sensitive then. And so he just lightly tickled her at first. She immediately opened up and began to moan slightly as he rubbed her in a circular motion. He looked up to her face and saw that her cheeks were burning a dark pink with arousal. He loved to look at her when she was in such a state of pleasure. Soon enough Amanda felt close and she began to raise her hips to grind against his hand.

"Noooooo……" Terrence pulled away and pushed her down. "You don't get to cum unless I tell you,"

"You always say that!" she laughed.

"I mean it this time!" And something about the look in his eyes showed that he meant it.

Meanwhile the sheriff was having a difficult time trying to control his urges. More than anything he wanted to jump on top of her and plough himself into her over and over again until he felt the sweet and intense satisfaction of releasing himself inside of her. But to show such weakness would ruin the illusion of being dominant. He needed to show her that he was calm and collected, aloof even so that she would want to submit to him even more. Playing hard to get sure could be fun, if not a really hard task when you had a woman as perfect and gorgeous as Amanda lying before you naked.

Terrence felt the bulge in his pants. His penis was pushing hard against the fabric and he wanted to release it. To pull it out and stroke it hard up and down and spray his seed all over her as she lay immobile. But of course he wouldn't do that. This was an exercise of control and so he just try to put it at the back of his mind for now. He knew that if he let the heat build-up inside him for long enough the climax would be the best ever.

He moved over and lightly stroked her stomach knowing full well that it was her most ticklish spot. He laughed as she squirmed and giggled underneath his touch. Next he circled figure of eight movements around her breasts with his fingers and before long they were too much to resist. Climbing up onto the bed he sat astride her waists and felt the frailness of her body beneath him. He leaned down and lightly flicked a nipple with his tongue but it wasn't enough. He cupped her breast in his mouth and sucked hungrily until it hurt her and she groaned. He knew it was turning her on and so he sat beside her, one hand between her legs and his mouth clamped around a nipple. Biting down on her hard he felt the torrent of wetness that was seeping out of her sex and onto his hand.

He pushed in a finger pressed up to hit her g spot. She screamed and flung her head back, crying for more. Next he slid in another finger and pushed over and over as he kissed her entire body. She was screaming wildly, trying to spread her legs wider but unable to because of the chains. Terrence kept moving inside of her as he placed his thumb on her clitoris and rubbed. The combination of the sensations was phenomenal and Amanda screamed louder and louder. She was about to climax and Terrence knew it but this time he was going to keep his word.

"You're not allowed to cum until I say so," he said.

It was of course an almost impossible task and as Amanda felt the torrent of pleasure rush through her she felt that she might explode. But she didn't want to displease her master and so she tried to distract her mind from what was happening below. As Terrence pleasured her pussy over and over she counted the floorboards, tried to spell her name backwards and even said her times tables in her head. It worked for a short while at least and she was able to stave off an orgasm. But that was until Terrence started to talk and it tilted her over the edge.

"That's my girl, cum for me baby cum for me. I wanna feel that sweet pussy cum. I wanna feel your juice all over my hand. I wanna see you cum so much,"

"Am I allowed to now?"

"Yeah sweetheart, you're allowed,"

And she finally let herself go and shook violently as she screamed. She had never felt a pleasure like it and it tore straight through her as the chains jangled as she moved. To her surprise though a completely new and unexplainable sensation ripped through her too and she squirted but so much harder than befor. The sight pleased Terrence so much that he felt he might orgasm right there without even touching himself.

Amanda fell back onto the bed. More than anything she wanted to wrap her arms around the sheriff and hug him hard. Mainly because she wanted to thank him for bringing her such pleasure but also because she needed his comfort. She looked down at her body and for the first time felt very vulnerable, lying there naked with the chains covering her body.

"You're incredible," Terrence rasped as he brushed a finger over her clitoris. She was still wildly sensitive and as he did so she shuddered and tried to pull away. "Not quite ready for round two?" he smirked.

"Not yet," she shook her head but her eyes said *give me a minute I'm almost ready again.*

"Well I guess you deserve a rest," Terrence sat down on the edge of the bed again and lit a cigarette.

Amanda thought it a filthy habit she could never take up but there was something she had always liked about the way Terrence smoked. It made him look like a rebel or some sort of outlaw. The way he gripped hold of one with his rough hand made him look manly and when he smoked it always made his jaw tense, accentuating its squareness and masculinity.

The sheriff blew smoke out into the room and Amanda watched it dance in the flickers of the candlelight. It appeared to bring a haze of mystery to the room that was only exaggerated when Terrence began to speak.

"Can I tell you a story Amanda?"

She nodded. He exhaled lazily and slumped a little. It looked as though the story he bore was a heavy one.

"So let me start. When I was a kid... Actually not much younger than you are now I was out on the lake, you know the one not far from here? Well anyway I was there with ma grandpa, a nice bug burly chap he was with a heart of gold..."

He began his tale and Amanda watched him speak seriously. She wondered where he was going and she looked into his eyes as deeply as possible to try and get to bottom of this mysterious man.

"Yeah my grandpa was a good guy," Terrence continued. "So we were out fishing on the lake and I was bored outta my mind I can tell ya," he chuckled to himself. "So I decided to excuse myself. I asked the old man if he could drop me off on the shore so I could go for a walk and the bumbling old guy agreed, though he was pretty cranky about bein' left alone," that chuckle again. "So anyhow I hopped out of the little boat that we were sailing in and up onto the banks of the lake. I really had to take a leak you know so I wondered up to a tree. And I was just standing there, taking a piss when I hear this noise and think *Shit! Someone's caught me!* Which is weird cos like... who cares about getting caught pissing,"

"Anyway I can't see anyone so I just keep going but then I hear it again. It's someone humming. Like a lady humming a tune while she's cooking dinner or somethin' like that. I pop my head around the tree and then there she is. All lovely and soft, pale and curvy... so much like you,"

Terrence left his words hanging enigmatically as he blew out the last of his cigarette.

"So... who was she?" Amanda asked.

"Well I have no idea! As I watched her I saw that she was lying there in the sun having a pleasant time and I didn't want to disturb her. It was a scorchin' day too! Really hot as hell and as I looked closer I realized that the lady was naked! Just naked! Sunbathing in between the trees by the lake. I scuffled in closer as quietly as I could because I'd never seen a naked lady before, not even in pictures. I mean once a kid at school drew in the dirt what he told us was boobs but you know...just kid stuff. So anyway I'm crouched down in the bushes getting a good look at this real pretty lady. She was the most beautiful thing I'd ever seen and I remember the profound moment....the very moment that I felt turned on. I looked her body up and down over and over because I just couldn't take my eyes off of her. She was divine.

So like a dumb kid I started jackin' off right there in the bushes. And then suddenly she just stops humming,"

"Oh no! Did she see you?" Amanda was fully enthralled by the story now and was desperate to hear more.

"She did. And she turned to look right at me,"

Amanda gasped, "What did she do? Did she scream?"

"She did nothing of the sort. In fact she turned to me and just like that she opened her legs right up and showed herself to me. I nearly fainted I can tell you that. And as I finished she just closed her legs and began to hum again as if nothing had happened,"

"Good God! What a woman!"

"She was certainly a strong woman,"

They both laughed.

"But anyhow that was the moment that for the first time in my life I felt truly alive sexually! It has been a moment I have struggled to recreate, especially the intensity. That has been almost impossible to copy. And believe me I've tried. Over the years I've been with many women hoping to get that sexual thrill that I had on that day when I was 17… but it never happened. But that was until I met you,"

And the silence returned to the room. It was, to Amanda, the most peculiar story she had ever been told and as she lay in the candlelight with the chains weighing her down she felt as though she was in a very surreal moment. She pondered why Terrence would have told her such a strange story but then it dawned on her that he was trying to be open and honest like he wanted her to be with him. He was trying to share an insight into his psyche as a reward for her being good to him. She felt that the very least she could do was to return the favour.

"You know I have a story of my own too!"

"Oh yeah?" Terrence looked to her with a surprised look on his face, his eyes wide with curiosity.

"Yeah! A time when I first felt sexually alive. Would you like to hear it?"

"Well yeah! Don't waste any more time, tell me!"

"Ok so…" she hesitated the moment she began to speak because she soon realized that she had never told a single person about this and she blushed. "So I was about the same age as you when I was at school one day. We had this old rickety math's teacher, Mr Bolder. Urgh… he was just the meanest guy you could ever meet. He'd throw anyone in detention for any reason at all but most of all his favorite punishment was the belt,"

Terrence realized what was going through her mind and he smiled as he nodded. "Oh! I see… Please tell me more,"

"Yeah so I was always a good girl. I have never been in trouble my whole time through high school but I had watched other kids get punished plenty of times. Lots of the girl would cry when Mr Bolder hit their hands with the belt. In fact I remember one girl in particular fainted when one day she hadn't done her homework and was ordered to the front of the glass. But you know… she was an odd one,"

Amanda laughed at the memory and her voice brought joy to Terrence who always had loved the sound of her when she was happy.

"So after a while I noticed that I really like to watch other kids get hit. I don't know why and for a long time I felt like I must have been a sick girl or something, you know sick in the head! But the more I tried to be a decent person and stop enjoying it the more I wanted to see. It was a feeling that just bubbled out of me! It didn't even matter who the kid was as long as Mr Bolder was shouting at them to place their hands out front. And he had a real knack at making it more painful than the other teachers, or so everyone said anyway. He'd make you hold out your hands, palm down and he'd really focus on getting that belt to hit all the little bumps of your bones and knuckles. My friends would be walking around with lumps the size of conkers on their fingers after he was finished,"

"But it was mostly the noise that I liked. The only way I can describe it is that it was like my ears were having an orgasm before the rest of me was; that swooshing sound followed by the smack, it was just divine. So each time I watched someone being taken up to the front of the class and belted I would close my eyes and just love the sound,"

"But the specific time when it all came to a head was when my best friend Janey was having boy troubles. She was sat next to me and would sporadically burst into tears because she was so lovesick. I was trying to comfort her and talk to her to make her calm but it infuriated Mr Bolder. The first time I just got some terse words of warning but the second time he caught me talking he leapt up out of his chair and smacked his hand hard on the desk. It made everyone in the class jump and then he shouted my name and gestured with that bony finger of his for me to walk up to the front. But I wasn't scared. I wasn't scared at all. In fact I was looking forward to it and had been for months. I had always wished that someday I would get to be at the receiving end of that swooshing and smacking,"

"So what was it like?" Terrence was dying to hear a happy ending.

"Well… it stung so much but at the same time it felt like a great comfort. For the rest of the day I kept looking at my red raw hands and smiling. When I got home I rubbed the soreness of my skin against the bed covers to make the stinging come back and it was beautiful,"

"You're a very strange and perfect girl Amanda," Terrence smiled and leaned forward to kiss her.

"I'm happy you think so," she kissed the end of his nose.

"So how about it?" Terrence picked up his belt from the end of the bed and started whipping it on the floor so that Amanda could hear that noise again. "You like that?"

She nodded. "Yeah…. Come 'ere,"

Terrence moved closer and brushed his hand across her thigh. "This would make a nice spot to spank,"

Amanda was begging him with her eyes to slap her with the belt and she thought her heart would beat out of her chest with the excitement. She started to blush and grow hot almost as if she were having a panic attack but it was the increase of anticipation merged with the torture of waiting that was having such an effect on her. She wanted to be hit and she wanted to be hit right now!

"Please! Just do it!" she cried.

SMACK!

Terrence reined the belt down on her thigh brutally and it stung so much at first that Amanda's ears were ringing. The pain was such a shock that it was almost too much to comprehend but then that hot sensation began to spread and she felt real joy. The heat of the pain mixed with the heat of her sex and she had never felt so aroused.

"Touch it," she said.

And Terrence fingered the hot, red skin of her thigh. It had made the perfect belt shaped indentation and he felt terribly guilty for hurting her but at the same he revelled in seeing her so happy and aroused.

"It isn't too much?" he asked with concern in his voice.

"Not at all! I want more!"

"Are you sure?"

She nodded eagerly again.

"Ok," Terrence picked the belt back up and SMACK! This time he hit the other thigh and Amanda screamed loudly. It was a cry of both pain and pleasure and Terrence grew so hard at hearing her voice. "You like that?"

"Uhuh!"

"What about here?" and he smacked the belt down on her breast.

She screamed loudly and yelled. "Again! Do it harder!"

And he did and the pain was exquisite to Amanda who was writing beneath the chains.

"I think that's enough now," said Terrence as he put the belt down.

"No! More!"

"I think you're forgetting that I'm in charge here," he laughed.

"You're such a tease!" Amanda was so infuriated that her words sounded more like primal grunts.

"I think it's my turn now. I can't keep it in any longer," said Terrence as he lifted his shirt off.

Amanda adored watching him undress and thought the musculature of his body was almost like a work of art. The way the muscles moved beneath his skin and rippled was incredible and she loved to watch the movement as he contracted the muscles around his back and shoulders. To Amanda he was like a god and she looked up to him in awe as he stripped naked.

He stood proudly in front of her with his penis in his hand. Making light motions at first he stroked his hand up and down but quickly stopped.

"I can't... I'm so close already,"

"I want to touch you so much," said Amanda as she realized the hindrance of confinement for the first time.

She desperately wanted to reach out and place him in her mouth as she worked on him with her hands but of course she couldn't. Out of all the things Terrence had done to her over the course of the evening this was the most torturous, keeping her hands away from him.

"I need you so much!" he gasped as he climbed on top of her.

"Do it!" she cried. "Please!"

And so Terrence lay down on top of her and kissed her gently.

"Are you ready?"

"Yes!" Amanda couldn't have wanted him more in her life.

He hesitated for a moment, wondering on how long it would take him to orgasm inside of her and he worried that it really wouldn't be very long at all. He looked into her eyes and saw the way she looked at him and it made up his mind quickly. Plunging into her rapidly and deeply he thrust inside of her over and over as hard as his body would allow. Both of them climaxed immediately and screamed loudly as their bodies shook in unison.

"Fuck!" Terrence shouted as his face grew red. "Oh fuck..... fuck...." He struggled to regain his breath.

After a long while he eventually rolled off of her and immediately unfurled all of the shackles. Mostly because he thought she would want to be free but also because he wanted to hold her properly. He unshackled her and flung the chains to the ground lazily.

"Finally...." He whispered as they cuddled in close.

Amanda lifted the sheets up over their bodies and once again they were just a regular couple in love.

"You're amazing," she smiled and felt the stubble on his cheeks with her delicate fingers.

"You too... You know I love you very much don't you?"

"Of course I do... and I love you too,"

The couple lay quietly in luxury for a moment before they both fell asleep satisfied and in love.

CHAPTER 18

"Well ain't you looking happier than a bride on her wedding day," Tony said sarcastically as Terrence entered the station.

"Ha….. hah….." was all the sheriff replied. "Ain't I always happy to be here?"

They both burst out laughing as Terrence took a seat at his desk.

"Say… How long have you and Amanda been courting?"

"Hmmm…. Well when you put it like that it sounds pretty formal," Terrence scratched his chin.

"Well ain't it?"

"Er…. Well yeah… I guess. It's been months now… many happy months," he felt himself blush as he cast his mind back over the happiness of the last year of knowing the girl.

"So you think you'll make it official soon?" Tony inquired.

"What do you mean….*official*?" Terrence squint his eyes at his deputy to try and gauge what he meant.

Tony swallowed nervously and looked at the floor. "You know…get married…." he trailed off mumbling, he'd said too much.

"Married??? You mean like playing happy families like everythin' is just all normal and hunky dory?"

"Well ain't it?"

"NO! I mean it was once… I had a wife… Evangeline…"

Tony knew it was a touchy subject and so just remained silent and made his excuses.

"Sorry sheriff, I was just askin', and he strode out of the building to attend something important he'd made up on the spot.

The truth was he just hated confrontation and Tony felt angry as he descended the front steps of the station. Who the hell did Terrence think he was? Amanda was a nice girl; smart, funny, beautiful and young if not somewhat naïve so why wouldn't the sheriff just god damn marry her. If Tony had even half the chance to do so he'd jump at it, she was the perfect girl. But that sheriff was a Pandora's Box of grief and unresolved issues and for every action that needed done Terrence had at least three abstract and confusing reasons why he wouldn't do the logical thing… Like move on with his life and marry Amanda.

He climbed on top his horse that was more like his best friend. Old Marlon was his name and the stallion had brought the deputy a lot of good company and support through the long days of patrolling the town of Wattsville, especially on quiet days like today when nothing was happening. He rode through the center of town, kicking up dust as Old Marlon trotted gracefully.

There was a saloon to his right, a well-known place called Sweaty Betty's. It was a hub of the criminal community and was as sordid as the name would suggest. Tony saw no harm in paying a visit like he did every week at some point. But the truth was that he had an eye for one of the saloon girls and her flaming, red hair and tiny waist always brought a smile to his face.

He swung the doors open and the patrons all turned to him at once but upon recognizing him they all turned back to their drinks disinterested. The clientele today appeared to be the usual mix of degenerate old folks and the criminally inclined. It was almost a home away from the station for Tony who was starting to grow fed up with having to fraternize with the seedy underbelly of Wattsville. What he would give to just sit down in beautiful restaurant with a smart girl for some intellectual conversation. He saw that happening as soon as he would see pigs flying though.

He sighed and sat at the bar. Holding up three fingers he signalled for scotch but the old lady behind the bar already knew that, it was his usual.

"You look tired deputy. You want me to send for Lianne?"

"Not yet Betty, not yet…" he held his forehead in his hand and squinted like he had a terrible headache.

"Say you're really not looking well deputy. I think you need something stronger!"

Tony nodded and Betty started to rummage in a drawer behind the bar. She was fetching him opium… a drug that was mostly frowned upon and which Tony would be ashamed of taking if anyone were to find out. But a man had to have his secrets… or so he kept telling himself anyway.

"So what's bringing you so much trouble?"

"I'm lovesick Betty,"

"Oh don't start! It's not that governess is it?"

"How did you know?" Tony looked up bemused.

"Oh God if I had a dime for every man that came in here lovesick because they were lusting after that hussy I'd be outta here and living it up somewhere with my toy boy,"

"She is NOT a hussy! How could you say that?"

Betty adjusted herself in her corset and laughed, showing her rotten teeth and smudged magenta lipstick. "That girl has been destroying the sacred bond of family I can tell ya, all that cavorting around with the sheriff. He should be ashamed of himself!"

"Look I don't wanna hear this! She's a sweet girl! And as much as I like her I'd urge the sheriff to marry her as soon as possible. He's my best friend and my boss after all and he could never find another girl like her… apart from Evangeline…"

Betty went silent at the deputy's stern words. The jealousy was etched on her face in the form of a grotesque grimace. All the women in the town were jealous of Amanda because not only was she the most beautiful girl that had ever set foot in Wattsville but she was also in bed with the sheriff, the man every girl in the town had eyes for.

"Well don't bother sending me an invite," scowled Betty as she walked away with a nastiness only reserved for men she was too old to get and too miserable to admit fancying.

An awkward silence reigned over the bar and all that could be heard was the sound of smoke exhaling from the patrons as they sat out their afternoon in a drunken haze. Tony pulled out some coins from him pocket and placed them down on the bar. He never knew why he tipped Betty when she always spoke to him like shit but that was the kind of person he was. He knew she'd had a hard life and so he was trying to show some kindness that maybe she'd never had before.

He was just about to leave when a voice came out of the darkness of a nearby corner and floated towards him on the breeze of a woodbine.

"She ain't the only one with a problem with that Boston Belle?" the voice sounded gritty and old, scarred even with the treacherous years of living in the country.

"And who are you?" asked the deputy as he squinted into the darkness.

"Just a concerned citizen of Wattsville…" came the enigmatic reply.

Tony walked out into the street with an anger inside of him. People could be so cruel and heartless. They'd rather see miserable people get married in an honourable union that displayed no love due to some ridiculous formality of honour than see two young people in love. He knew where to go next.

The church lay on top of the hill and was a great solace to Tony at times. He wasn't much of a God fearing man but he hoped that up there was someone that protected all of humanity. He knew that his Cherokee ancestors would have different ideas on the universe but he never found himself strictly following one theory. He did however love being in the church. Just being in such a holy place of peace brought him tremendous joy. He knew that somewhere, whoever God was, he was listening to him.

He purposely strode up the steps and happily entered the building. As always he was the only one in there at this time of day. The contrast between the harsh sunlight and the shadows of the church made his eyes hurt and his vision hazy. He sat for a little while just thinking, contemplating what the right thing to do was.

Eventually he walked slowly over to the display of candles that stood at the altar and listened to the sound of his footsteps as they echoed all around the building. All the candles were unlit but that was until he struck a match and set a wick on fire.

"Please God… If only one of my prayers ever comes true can it be this one? With all my heart please ensure that my two best friends live a long and happy life together,"

And he blew out the match and exited the building.

CHAPTER 19

"You're looking a little off there," Mrs Wheen, although wearing her glasses, was still squinting comically to look at Amanda.

"I'm fine really… I just wanted to come over to ask if you had any spare milk?"

"Oh of course," the old lady began to fidget around the kitchen in search of some. "But tell me, are you feeling ok?"

"Yes fine… I mean I think I had some sort of stomach sickness but I'm fine really,

Mrs Wheen didn't look convinced and she approached the girl as if she were fragile.

"Take a seat. Now let's check you over,"

Amanda sat down feeling a little bewildered because she didn't know what the old lady was fussing about. It was just a stomach big wasn't it? Mrs Wheen sat down beside her at the kitchen table and felt her brow.

"Hmmm…. Not too hot… but there is something different," she carried on with her peculiar inspection.

Amanda was starting to feel as though she were being treated by some sort of witch as Mrs Wheen began to prod her enigmatically while mumbling to herself. Eventually she asked the young girl to stand up before massaging her stomach with her turgid and bony fingers.

"If I'm not wrong I'd say you have yourself in a predicament,"

Amanda laughed at the seriousness of her tone and chuckled, "And what kind of predicament would that be?" she thought the old dear had gone nuts.

"Those rosy cheeks, swollen breasts and slightly podgy joints… not to mention your stomach problem," Mrs Wheen struggled to find the right words without offending the young governess. "If I'm not mistaken I'd say you're pregnant. A good few months in as well,"

Amanda staggered backwards and gasped. "Pregnant? How on earth would you know?" her voice was a mixture of both curious and sceptical.

"Believe me I've had seven of my own. I know what a pregnant body looks like?" and she set about retrieving the milk as if everything was normal.

Amanda however chased her into the pantry.

"Mrs Wheen? You really think so? I can't be!" she protested.

"And why's that? You've been intimate with Mr Evans haven't you?"

Amanda suddenly felt very naïve. Of course she had been having sex… but she was so caught up in the excitement of being in love that she never once worried about falling pregnant. And then another thought struck Amanda. How did Mrs Wheen know she had been sleeping with Terrence? On cue as if Mrs Wheen could hear her thoughts she answered.

"Everybody knows darling… but as long as you love each other I'm so very happy for the both of you. And that little Helen could do a lot worse than have you for a step mother. Now run along now. I believe you'll need to be sharing the good news with the sheriff," and she handed over the milk to Amanda.

That woman is a witch I'm sure of it, thought Amanda to herself as she left the old lady's house. *Does she really know I'm pregnant? Surely not…* and she went back home and tried her best to put Mrs Wheen's ramblings to the back of her mind. However it was an impossible feat and as she lay in bed next to her lover she gazed at him both lovingly and worryingly. What were they to do if it so happened she were with child? Would Terrence be happy? More than anything she panicked that he would leave her or send her packing back home as some sort of scarlet woman. Her parents would be devastated and they'd more than likely turn her away too. Thoughts began to race through her head over and over until they became so abstract amongst the chaos of her mind that she eventually drifted into a nightmare filled sleep.

~

When the couple awoke Amanda thought that she would have a nearly impossible task of keeping quiet about her worries. She always was terrible at keeping a secret and as she'd learned Terrence was always the eager detective and could read her like a book. She tried her best to avert eye contact and just tried to busy herself with Helen and the housework. Soon enough he left for work and was so consumed with what he had to do at the station that he never paid too much attention to her.

"The big wigs from up state are coming in today," he said solemnly as he banged the front door shut and Amanda breathed a sigh of relief.

However a little someone seemed to have inherited the detective gene.

"You're sick aren't you?" asked a very worried Helen who was pulling on her governess' skirts.

"And what makes you say that?" Amanda asked her suspiciously.

"Well you didn't eat breakfast this morning and I heard you being sick in the middle of the night,"

"Hmmmmm… You're right I've not been feeling very well. Would you care to escort me to the doctor's surgery like a good girl?"

Helen nodded.

Good, Amanda thought. This was the only was her worries could be settled properly.

~

"Yup a good few months in I'd say," the doctor confirmed her fears.

"But no! I just can't be!"

"Well unless our lord and saviour came down from the heavens and blessed you with a second baby Jesus then I must say that you are… and you know fine well how,"

Amanda had tears springing from her eyes as she sat up from the doctor's table. She nodded to show him that she really did know how it happened.

"But this is a nightmare! I never planned this at all!" her tears flowed more freely and her sobs became louder. "I just don't know what to do!" she was desperate. She absolutely adored children but she still had so much of her life she wanted to live before she created her own. She quickly felt very grown up and very stupid.

"Look all I can suggest," the doctor began to speak rather condescendingly through his moustache. "Is that you notify the gentleman… depending on what he says… we'll move on from there," and he said no more and just moved back to his desk and began scribbling his notes frantically. He didn't even say goodbye as a tearful Amanda left his office.

Helen was waiting for her in the reception room and she immediately looked terrified when she saw her governess' face.

"Are you ok miss?"

"Yes I'll be fine, just feeling a little poorly right now is all," and Amanda hurried her home.

She felt as though she would wear out the floors as she paced frantically. Terrence would be home soon and she'd have to tell him. He would have heard about her trip to the doctor's already, this town was a hub of gossipers and nobody kept themselves to themselves around here.

On time the sheriff came home with the most serious expression on his face.

"I've heard already Amanda. You don't need to tell me," he put down his hat at though it weighed a ton.

He walked with a sombre face to the kitchen where he poured himself a drink. Amanda noticed that he hadn't looked her in the eyes since his returned. Chances were he was just as devastated as she was. But she thought that somewhere in there he would have an ounce of tenderness. She approached him for a hug but he coldly pulled away. It felt cruel and harsh to her and so she left him alone with his thoughts. Venturing upstairs she lay on the bed of her old bedroom and cried. Next door she could hear the playful sounds of Helen and her toys and she wondered what it would be like to have another child in the house. She had seldom thought of herself as a mother but now that it was an inevitability she warmed to the idea. Thinking of a life growing inside of her that was precisely half her and half Terrence was a beautiful thought. She wondered it would look like. If it was a girl it was bound to be as beautiful as Helen and a boy would grow up to be strong like his daddy. Amanda caught herself day dreaming and stopped herself. What did she think she was doing? Here she was in an almighty bad situation and she was lying around romanticizing. She was going to find out what was happening right away.

She dried her tears with the cuff off her dress and marched downstairs. She found the sheriff on the porch blowing smoke out into the twilight.

"Can I sit next to you?" she asked carefully.

He nodded.

"So what are you thinking?" she inquired and tried to figure out what was on his mind by the look in his eyes.

"Oh God I mean I don't know Amanda. I never wanted another child. Never even thought about it,"

The words stung at her heart and she swallowed back tears. She didn't want him to see her as being weak. There was a long and eerie silence as Terrence said nothing. She had to admit that she was hurt he didn't ask her how she felt about it.

"I don't think it would be such a bad thing," she tried to reason.

"Oh really!" Terrence seemed appalled at her attitude.

"You think it's terrible don't you. Does this whole damn place know already?"

"Well of course! You fled the doctor's surgery in tears not to mention Mrs God damn Wheen has told just about everybody she's met over the last day,"

"I hate this place! I HATE IT! Why can't people mind their own business like back in Boston?" She was so furious that she yelled loudly, not noticing that Helen had come out to join them.

"Well if you hate this place so much why don't you just head on back to Boston then!" Terrence shouted louder. "I'm sure that family of yours will be so pleased to have their daughter back home once she's the size of a sow!"

The couple yelled back and forth taking turns to hurl insults. Meanwhile a tortured Helen stood in the middle feeling terribly upset. She loved these two people more than anything else in the world and to her it felt like her little universe was starting to unravel. She tried her best to get their attention.

"Daddy? Miss Amanda?" her tiny voice was eclipsed by the roaring of the adults.

Soon enough she started to feel very dizzy and as the yelling reached a crescendo Helen's vision became blurry and she promptly passed out. Both Amanda and Terrence hurried to her and held her tightly as she woke up. Her father especially was distraught.

"Princess?" he spoke softly as he brushed back the hair from her face.

"I'm ok daddy," the little voice came as the limp body in his arms came back to life.

"What happened?" asked Amanda. "You've not been unwell in such a long time," she was perplexed.

"Please stop arguing," was all Helen said before Terrence carried her inside to bed.

CHAPTER 20

"Well fuck… I don't know what to do," Terrence was pacing maniacally round the back of the station with a cigarette in his hand. Occasionally he'd suck on the end and absent mindedly blow out the smoke. Usually his bad habit always calmed him down but today it did nothing to placate his nerves.

Meanwhile Tony was sitting on a rock as he twiddled with his beard. Watching the sheriff in such a state of anxiety was making him panic too. He tried to see reason.

"Well… I mean I don't see why you can't be a family. Amanda is good with kids ain't she? I think she'd make a great mom!" he knew instantly that he had said the wrong thing.

Terrence flashed him a look of pure scepticism. "Well that's beside the point ain't it? I mean… we just can't be A FAMILY you know. I had a wife and a family once and that was that. I can't just have a nineteen year old girl as my wife! Not especially now she's pregnant out of wedlock. I'm the whole laughing stock of the town!" he buried his head in his hands. "What must people think of me? I'm supposed to uphold responsibility not abuse it,"

"What does it matter what the townsfolk think? They're just people like you and I! If you show me one single person in this town who hasn't done something wrong I'll show you a god damn wart hog with a bank account," and the deputy chuckled to himself. "Look. Seriously speaking… You're not just by boss you're my best friend. I want nothing more than to see you happy and I think that Amanda can bring you that happiness if you'd just let her. And if people talk well let 'em… no doubt they'll soon move on to another undeserving victim and they'll forget all about you! Listen… please. Just think about it," and he patted the sheriff on the back before heading back inside.

Terrence spent a long while sitting out amongst the tall grass and thinking. His deputy was always good at these things, at matters of the heart. And he knew that he was right. It was about time he moved on with his life and settled down with Amanda… and that child of hers that was inside her. But was it that easy? Throughout the day the more he thought about it the more he realized it was himself that he was afraid of. He was terrified if making a failure of himself as a husband but most of all he was terrified that Amanda would also die in childbirth like Evangeline. That's why he thought it would be easier to push her away before he lost her. It was a warped sort of logic but his mind felt all twisted up. As he left the station at the end of the day he thought he knew exactly what to do.

~

He found Amanda in the evening lying in their bed with a cold compress on her forehead.

"Still feeling rough?" he asked her.

"Like you wouldn't believe," she answered. "Been sick twice in the last hour," she sighed.

Terrence sat down beside her and held her hand tenderly.

"We need to talk," he spoke gruffly.

"We do," was all she said.

"Well I don't know where to start so I may as well just come out with it," he paused for a moment and swallowed back her nerves. "I think you should go…"

Amanda sat bolt upright in shock.

"Go? Go where? You're throwing me out because I'm pregnant?" she was both enraged and horrified! The thought of having to return to her family pregnant out of wedlock was destroying her. She'd rather kill herself than be so humiliated.

"I'm sorry but it's the right thing to do," Terrence spoke softly as though he was embarrassed of his own words.

"The right thing for who?" asked Amanda but she didn't need a reply.

And Terrence didn't speak either and so she got up and walked away before she made a fool of herself and cried like a child. She felt that she must move quickly. If she lingered in the house then saying goodbye would be too difficult and so she set about packing her things. She'd leave by sundown and make her way east. She didn't know where she was going and she didn't know how but she'd find a way. She had savings, her youth and a strong disposition. She could start a new life built on anger and she'd find her way eventually.

"Look there's no hurry for you to leave," Terrence tried to calm her down. "You can stay a little while longer."

"Nonsense! You want me gone now! That way you'll never have to worry about me or the baby, not ever!" she was seething as she flung clothes into a suitcase. "Besides if you wanted me to stay a little while longer you wouldn't have asked me to leave the very second you came home," she had a point and it left the sheriff speechless.

Amanda barged passed him in the hallway but as she approached Helen's bedroom she steadied herself.

"Pumpkin?" she popped her head around the door and saw the little girl playing on the floor with her toys.

Helen looked up joyfully at her. "Uhuh? Why are you crying?" she looked upset to see her governess so miserable. "Are you sick again?"

"Yes I'm afraid so… In fact I'm so terribly sick so I'm just going to dash outside quickly to visit the doctor but I'll be home soon. I promise," it was a despicable lie but she couldn't bear to tell the girl the truth.

"Oh! OK!" Helen resumed her play time and thought nothing more of her governess' words.

Amanda felt a pain beyond description as she bumped her suitcase down the stairs. Terrence called down after her but she was already at the front door.

"Don't leave yet Amanda! Please! We can talk this through!"

But the front door slammed and Amanda was already gone.

~

"So she just left?" Tony asked incredulously as he looked out the living room window into the darkness.

"Yup… just left. Just walked right out the door with her things," Terrence was beside himself with worry. "What have I done?" It was the second time in a day he was begging his deputy for advice.

"Well you did tell her to leave," Tony said rather flatly in an "I told you so" fashion.

"Yeah but I didn't mean it! I wasn't thinking straight I was just… Oh I dunno…. Just petrified!"

"Well if you'd just listened to me then you wouldn't be in this predicament now would you?" the deputy scalded Terrence. "Well I tell ya what. I'll head out on ma horse and see if I can find her. She couldn't have gone far on foot, not unless someone picked her up.

The thought hit Terrence like a bolt of lightning. What if someone had picked her up? Someone with insidious plans… He had been a sheriff long enough to know that some truly evil people existed on God's earth and that Amanda would be the perfect prey for them. He felt his stomach churn violently as Tony disappeared down the track on the top of Old Marlon.

CHAPTER 21

"That God damn idiot," Tony muttered to himself as he squinted in the dark. "What has he done?"

The deputy couldn't believe the situation he was in; riding on his horse through the darkness of a sleepy town looking for a runaway, pregnant girl. He rode around the town center for a long while hoping to just find her sitting in a sulk somewhere but he had no such luck. Next he tried the back roads thinking that she had wanted to find solace in visiting a neighbour. But as he arrived at each house they soon told him they hadn't seen her. He looked at the disdain in their eyes and took note of their snide comments. It made him angry and even more determined to find her. As a last resort he decided to check the church. He knew that if he were ever in trouble that's where he would head.

He left Old Marlon at the bottom of the steps and hurried up into the building. Candlelight glowed from within, beckoning to him with their peace. But all the deputy saw was empty pews and it left him feeling as empty as the church. He was naïve to think that a young girl would come here in times of need, if anything it was the last place she would be.

For the second time in such a short space of time Tony leant down before the candles at the altar. He lit one of the wicks and bowed his head.

"Please may she find safety…" he whispered before getting up with a heavy heart and heaving back outside to his horse.

~

The very moment Amanda had run away on foot with her heavy suitcase she had regretted acting so immaturely. She could have at least waited until morning and spent the night making some sort of plan. But the anger inside her wouldn't let her and so she now walked the dirt track that took her further out into the country. She felt that nausea creep up inside her once more and suddenly felt exhausted. Unable to figure out how long she could walk she began to panic. Should she just give up and head back to Terrence? No. Absolutely not because he was the one who suggested throwing out a woman after he got her pregnant.

She placed her suitcase down on its side and sat on top of it.

"Urgh…." She flung her head into her hands. "I've nowhere to go and nobody," and she began to sob uncontrollably.

But then a noise caught her attention and she looked down the road. She thought at first that her mind was playing tricks on her but then she saw that it was most definitely a man on a horse.

"Terrence?" she whispered. Maybe he'd changed his mind and after becoming riddled with guilt had decided to come and find her.

But as the man came closer she saw that it wasn't the sheriff.

"Who is that?" she struggled to see.

The horse she certainly didn't recognize. It was the most pristine white with a silver mane. It walked in the most distinguished and proud manner and in no way could have come from Wattsville.

"A maiden in distress I see!" a booming voice came from atop the horse.

Amanda looked up to see a diamond jawed, gentleman with glistening blue eyes.

"In a spot of trouble are we?"

He asked as he reached down a hand. She took it meekly and felt the bizarre compulsion to curtsy.

"In trouble like you wouldn't believe sir," she said in between sobs.

"Very well! I couldn't possibly say no to a tearful face like that, hop on!" his voice was a mixture of elegant and arrogant. A man you just didn't say no to.

For a moment Amanda struggled to get her trunk up onto the horse but once in place they set off. She noticed that her suitcase was sitting on his coat tails and that her view was mostly obstructed by his enormous top hat. Wondering who this man was she tried to compose a suitable question that would give her an answer without her sounding either suspicious or ungrateful.

"So... Do you come across many maidens in distress?"

"Oh countless ladies yes," he said and Amanda could tell he was smiling.

"And you always stop to help?"

"Oh of course! It has been in my upbringing after all to be a good Samaritan,"

She decided that the man was nice and trustworthy, his voice oozed money and his relaxed demeanour promoted a sense of safety within the lost girl.

"Well madam my name is Vincent, but Vinnie to my friends,"

"I'm Amanda," she said.

"Lovely name! I once knew a girl named Amanda... a gorgeous creature with porcelain skin. She did however meet an unfortunate end," and he didn't care to elaborate.

Amanda felt a little uneasy at his last remark and so tried to change the subject.

"So where are you heading?"

"East," was all he replied. "To the East," he repeated rather enigmatically.

"Is that where your family are from?"

"In a way..." that mystery again.

To settle her nerves Amanda decided that maybe he was just a very private person or at least just tired. It was after all late at night. She did notice though that he hadn't asked her where she was going… so where was he taking her?

"So you have somewhere to stay for the night?" she asked.

"Oh yes! Not far from here. Say how about you stay at mine for the night. We'll have a nice drink and in the morning we can set about sorting out your troubles,"

That seemed very reasonable to the girl who beamed: "That would be great! Thank you! But….. Didn't you say you were heading east?" she was confused again.

"I am…" again he didn't care to elaborate.

"I noticed your accent is definitely not a Wyoming one…" again she tried to change the subject.

"It is not… most definitely not…"

"If I wasn't mistaken I'd say you had a hint of the European in you," she tried to prod for more information.

"You would be correct," he said no more.

And so they rode in silence through the darkness of the cornfields for what seemed to Amanda like hours. Her mind flitted over the last day and she wondered if Terrence had noticed yet that she was gone forever. Chances are he didn't care anyway. Or so she thought… She felt deeply sad at the thought of Helen waking up the morning without her governess being there to dress her, to make her breakfast and to sing her songs as she played. Her tears began to fall again and make little popping sounds on the saddle.

"I say is that tears I hear again?" Vincent asked without a second of hesitation.

Amanda was shocked at his intuition. He acted as though it was a sound he had heard many times before.

"Yes… tears… But I wish I could stop shedding them,"

"Oh don't worry. Soon enough you won't be able to cry anymore,"

That uneasiness in Amanda's gut again. Who was this man? She began to realize that it was likely she wasn't in the safest of situations. They rode for a little while longer in silence until a barn came up over the hill and Vincent began to slow his horse down. He pulled out his pocket watch and tried to read the clock face in the moonlight.

"Bang on midnight! Marvellous," he declared although he didn't explain why he was so happy.

He rode the horse up towards the barn and took a left down a narrow lane. Soon enough Amanda saw that a little house lay behind the barn. It was well kept, surrounded by flowers and a homely light glowed from the inside. It looked warm and safe in there and Amanda felt the desperate need to go inside and find somewhere comfortable to fall asleep.

"Right well here we are!" Vincent leapt of the horse and helped Amanda to get down.

She felt stiff from being on the horse for so long and tried to stretch her legs.

"Yes that was quite the long journey," the man spoke as he watched Amanda bend over to touch her toes.

"It was," she said.

Amanda looked up and in the pale moonlight she could finally see the true beauty of the horse she was just on. It almost looked iridescent in the silver light.

"This is the most beautiful horse I have ever seen!"

"She's a smasher alright!" Vincent said as he patted the side of the horse's stomach. "Yes my fair lady Anne of Cleves is a tremendous travel companion. A real treasure,"

"She most certainly is!" Amanda agreed. "And just the most beautiful silvery, white, a really rare specimen,"

"Oh she is and I just love her so much. Except this perfect shade of white can be such a nuisance at times. It's impossible to get the blood stains out of," and he bellowed a laugh that came straight from his gut.

It shocked Amanda who took a step back horrified. She was certain that she misheard him or at least prayed that he did. But she didn't have enough time to contemplate what he said because he quickly held her by the arm and led her towards the house.

"Right well... let's get you inside. It's getting cold out," and he picked up her suitcase to make it easier for her to walk.

The man chapped the door rather dramatically and Amanda was nervous in guessing who would answer. She was however immediately pleased when a beautiful and homely girl answered the door. She couldn't have been much older than herself and had the most beautiful blonde hair that tumbled down passed her waist.

"My Lulu!" the man sang and kissed the girl on the cheek. "Lucy, we have a visitor for the night. Please can you see that she has somewhere comfortable to stay for the night? You can set up the guest bedroom,"

"Of course," said the girl Lucy and she took the Amanda by the hand and led her inside.

"Oh dear you're so cold!" the girl spoke in an accent that wasn't too different from Amanda's. "Have you been stuck outside long?"

"Just a few hours," said Amanda who was perplexed at the girl's friendliness. "Are you used to having strangers in your house?" she asked as Lucy showed her the way to a bedroom on the first floor.

"Oh all the time! Daddy always brings girls back here," the statement was intended to be innocent but Amanda couldn't help but hear sinister implications.

Lucy set about making the bed and Amanda was eager to help. Once finished, Lucy lit a fire and some more candles before leaving.

"If you're not too tired you can come meet me downstairs for some midnight nibbles?" the offer seemed friendly and so Amanda accepted.

"I'll be down in a moment," she smiled and Lucy smiled back before leaving Amanda to get settled in.

A few minutes later the governess was descending the stairs of the house and finding her way to the kitchen. A warm fire blazed and the room smelled like cinnamon. Lucy was sat the table with two glasses of warm milk and a plate of cookies.

"They're my grandma's recipe," she said as she pushed the plate towards Amanda.

"Lovely!" said the governess before taking one and nibbling delicately on the edges.

"You look as confused as the rest of them," said Lucy.

"What do you mean?"

"My Daddy's always bringing stray girls back here but it's not what you think. He's a kind man…" she drank from her glass while she gathered her thoughts. "Well I may as well tell you… but it's quite the story so make sure you're comfortable.

Dear God this entire family is a mystery wrapped up in an enigma, Amanda thought to herself. All she wanted was a safe place to sleep for the night before she could organize herself in the morning but fate had obviously sucked her up into something more interesting.

~

The night had grown thick with misery as Terrence sat faithfully on the porch. He was sure that at any moment he would see Amanda return, suitcase in hand and tears in her eyes, but of course she didn't. As the morning hours rolled in Terrence guessed that she had made up her mind, she was gone for good. However that sadness had been replaced with something far worse, a stomach churning terror at the thought that she had come to harm.

In a moment of madness Terrence grabbed his shotgun and walked out into the night but as he looked up and down the main road he saw that there was nothing to chase. He walked back to the house with a strong feeling that he was losing his mind. As he entered the house he felt the strong compulsion to cry and a small tear even managed to escape from the corner of his eye. But he stopped himself quickly because sheriffs don't cry, especially not over a girl.

He walked into the kitchen and poured himself a drink. As he looked into the almost empty bottle he vowed that if Amanda were to return to him he would stop his daily drinking. Hell he would even stop smoking! In fact he would do anything to have her back.

A noise came from upstairs and Terrence thought for a moment that it was her but then he realized it was just the creaking of Helen's bed as she turned in her sleep. But every sound that came to him sounded like Amanda and he had to remind himself that she was gone… and it was his fault.

~

"My Daddy," Lucy began as she chewed down on a cookie. "He's a lovey gentleman, really… a true prince. He's never been the same since my mama died though,"

"Oh I'm so sorry to hear that," Amanda touched Lucy's hand and nodded to show her compassion.

Lucy nodded back solemnly. "It was cholera, it took her quickly but it was for the best, she didn't have too long to suffer like other folk,"

"Your father must really miss her,"

"Oh he does! That's why he keeps bringing girls back here to care for them. All sorts of girls I tell ya… all running away from their troubles," she gave Amanda a little embarrassed look, she didn't mean to offend her.

"Well it was so kind of him. I would have been in real trouble if it weren't for him,"

"I'm sorry if he said anything out of the ordinary, he has a real odd sense of humour… plays up on it well," Lucy laughed.

"Well I did wonder! He said your horse was difficult to get the blood stains out of," Amanda giggled.

"Well that's not a joke. That's true!"

Amanda gasped and felt her heart race.

"I'm joking!" laughed Lucy! "That old chestnut is a favourite of his. He should really stop winding people up some day or he'll give some poor soul a heart attack,"

"Well he's quite the character,"

"Yeah…" Lucy sighed and poured another glass of milk for her guest.

"The jokes… the drama of it all… it helps him cope. Grief can do strange things to a person,"

"It certainly can," said Amanda as she thought back to her peculiar ride out here.

"Say his voice… he's not from here is he?"

"He was born in Germany but came here when he was 20! Plays up on the accent, makes him sound enigmatic,"

They both laughed.

"Well I guess you'll be tired,"

"Exhausted," yawned Amanda.

"Well you're welcome to stay as long as you want. My mama was a good lady and would have loved the idea of us taking care of people in need. Make yourself at home,"

"You're really so very generous. Thank you,"

And Amanda headed up to bed. It felt comfortable and homely in her guest room. Everything was girly and tastefully furnished. Her bed covers were her favorite shade of baby blue and there were even flowers on the dresser. The room smelled of lavender and clean laundry and it was beautifully warm. She was as comfortable as she could possibly be but something was missing, a resolution or some closure. As her eyes weighed down heavily she wondered what Terrence would be thinking back home. He was probably glad to see her gone. A rage burnt inside her as she thought of him telling her to leave. How dare he? She found it hard to sleep thinking about how vile he was. She had given herself to him in every way imaginable. She had surrendered her soul to him, her sense of control, her body and her mind but most of all she had given him her heart. As she lay awake she felt as though she had been trampled by heartbreak and she finally admitted to herself that she was desperately miserable without Terrence. She sobbed heavily until there were no more tears and fell into a deep, dream filled sleep.

~

The sun rose up over Wattsville as the morning broke but Terrence hadn't slept a wink. In fact he felt more awake than ever as he worried wildly about Amanda. Soon enough Helen would wake up and she'd be distraught if she found out her governess was gone. The shotgun was still by his side on the porch and as he looked down to it he wondered why he'd got it out in the first place. He had to be down at the station in a few hours and he had no idea where Helen would go. Mrs Wheen? He didn't really know her as well as Amanda did, it would seem awkward and rude. More than anything he hoped that he wouldn't have to take her to the station. As long as he lived he'd make sure that she'd never have to be witness to such an establishment of human degeneracy. He vowed that she'd always be a princess.

As Terrence went inside the house he heard the bed springs bounce again but he prayed that she was still asleep. He had no such luck though because next he heard the sound of her little bare feet walking quickly down the hallway above him.

"Miss Amanda?" she called.

"No sweety, come downstairs!" Terrence yelled quickly so that she wouldn't go into his bedroom and find that it was empty.

What she did though was worse because she walked into Amanda's bedroom and immediately saw that all her belongings were gone. She ran down the stairs completely panic stricken.

"Where are her clothes?? Where are her things? She's still here ain't she?" the little girl sounded desperate.

"She's just gone to run an errand," Terrence lied terribly and Helen could hear his voice waver as he spoke.

"Where is she?" was all she asked, she didn't want excuses she wanted answers.

"I told you, she's running errands. Now go get dressed,"

Terrence looked at his daughter as she stood on the stairs with fury in her eyes. She may have only come up to slightly above his knee but she was more intimidating that anyone else because he actually cared about her feelings and that meant he didn't always get his way.

"She's gone isn't she?" Helen screamed but she desperately hoped that she hadn't guessed right.

Terrence meanwhile couldn't lie to his daughter any longer. She was such a beautiful and ethereal creature standing before him and all he wanted to do was please her, make her happy. But he knew fine well that the moment he nodded his head her world would collapse.

"Yes pumpkin, she left last night," he nodded but he wished there was something else he could say.

Helen's tortured scream was so visceral that it almost came out as a howl. Terrence was shocked to see her so loud because since she was a baby she had never acted out. He would often see infants misbehave in the quintessential toddler tantrums that their parents had become accustomed too but Helen was never like that. She was an angel and always so sweet and quiet.

But in this moment she was flailing her arms and legs to the ground in the worst temper her father had seen.

"I want Amanda!!!" her tears were running down her bright red face, dampening the top of her nightgown.

Terrence went to her and tried to calm her down. He scooped her up in his big bear arms and held her tight.

"Shhhhh......She'll be back soon. She'll be home soon," he prayed that she would.

But his words were doing nothing to placate the hurt that was inside his little girl. She was such a fragile creature, so innocent and delicate that any notion of change brought about terrible anxiety. And Amanda should have known that! How could she have left knowing that Helen would miss her this much? He was angry now, not worried. If only he could turn back time.Instead of asking her to leave the moment he was home he would hold her instead. Tell her he loved her and kiss her softly. He'd tell her of his plans for the baby.

"Your old bedroom could be the nursery?" he'd suggest and she'd smile in agreement.

Then they would begin to think of names.

"How about Tony for a boy?" he would ask her and she'd beam thinking it was a great idea.

He would be there for every moment of her pregnancy and he would make sure it was easy for her. Terrence cursed himself for being immature despite the fact that he was a grown man. More than anything he had wanted to come home and ask her to marry him. He knew it was the right thing to do and it would have made him and Helen happier than they could imagine. But he had acted out of fright, he was terrified at what people would say and in a moment of madness he had made a rash decision and made her leave... and all because he was too scared to confront his feelings. He was too scared to lose her like he had his first wife.

As he sat on the stairs with a sobbing Helen in his arms he felt the black mist of a broken heart drift through him.

"I hope she comes back soon!" Helen cried.

"I hope so too!" her father felt as though he was also on the verge of crying.

"Daddy I don't feel so well,"

He looked down to Helen and placed his hand to her brow. She was pale and in a cold sweat and the more she cried the more she began to panic.

"I can't breathe!" she gasped and dug her tiny fingers into Terrence's arm. "My head is dizzy!" she cried harder.

"Please try to calm down sweetheart. If you take it easy you'll feel better I promise. You're just panicking,"

But his words were doing nothing to console her and she quickly began to hyperventilate.

"Daddy!" she cried louder. "I can't breathe!" and she became so ghostly pale that Terrence wondered whether she was even in his arms anymore.

As he bent down to kiss her forehead he noticed that she had gone limp in his arms. She had fainted.

~

Amanda woke up thinking that she was in bed with Terrence. She rolled over to hold onto a vacant space beside her and she soon remembered where she was. Very quickly she sobered up from the drama of the previous night and felt incredibly guilty. Not at leaving Terrence, he deserved what he got, but for lying to Helen. No doubt the little girl that meant so much to her would have found her gone already.

For a moment she began to think that she should hurry home if only for a moment to see to her princess. But she'd already said her goodbyes and so she wasn't going back on her word. Underneath her room Amanda could hear the sound of breakfast being made; pots and pans and the noise of sizzling meat. And then she heard that cheery voice of the man who picked her up. He was joyfully saying goodbye to his daughter and Amanda jumped out of bed and walked to the window to see him leave. She watched him walk up the track from the front door and head over to the stables. *He was such a peculiar man…* She thought, *albeit a very kind one.*

She stared out the window for a while as if looking out to the fields would bring answers to her problems. Now that she had her freedom and found somewhere to stay for a short while she felt a deep relief but the added freedom gave her extra fear. The more she tried to reason that running away was for the best she couldn't help but feel she was going against the grain of her instincts. A gentle tapping came from her door and Lucy popped her head round.

"Good morning!" she sang.

"Morning Lucy!"

"Did you sleep well?"

"Oh yeah! This room is beautiful!"

"Thank you. Actually we've had quite a few guests in here over the last couple years and well… they've always seemed to make it their own.

"So you really do have a lot of girls stay here?"

"Like you wouldn't believe, there are so many young girls like yourself that run away from home for whatever reason. We're just happy to get to them before danger does,"

"You're a very special family," smiled Amanda.

"Thank you…" Lucy answered feeling a little awkward. "Well there's breakfast if you want any," and she smiled again and left Amanda to herself.

As Amanda joined her new friend for breakfast in the kitchen she felt terrible.

"Are you ok?" asked Lucy as she piled food up on Amanda's plate.

"I think so…" she wasn't sure.

"Well… you look troubled,"

"I think I should go home,"

"Well as long as you have a safe home to go to then maybe it's worth heading back to work things out," she offered an option.

"Maybe…" Amanda bit on the end of some sausage. "I miss my little girl!"

"Oh I didn't realize you had a daughter. How lovely,"

"Well I don't really. She's my step daughter in a way…" she said no more.

"I'm sure she's adorable,"

"I've made a terrible mistake," Amanda blurted out. "I need to go home right now," tears began to spill from her cheeks. "I need to go home to Helen!"

"Listen just calm down… Calm down… Take a deep breath.

"I'm ok….I'm ok…." Amanda tried to calm herself down and she sat at the table with her head in her folded arms. "I think I've just been very immature and silly. I should have stayed,"

"Well if your heart tells you to leave then that is the right thing to do. You wanna know what I think?"

Amanda looked up with bleary eyes and nodded at Lucy.

"I think…" Lucy began. "That we come into people's lives for a reason… and when we meet a special person we have to hold onto them…"

Amanda looked back up to the girl to try and understand what she meant.

"What I'm saying is…" Lucy carried on. "Is that when the perfect person lands on your doorstep you don't let them leave so easily,"

The governess felt uneasy. What was the girl talking about?

"I'm sorry Lucy… I'm obviously sillier than I thought. What do you mean?"

There was a strange glint in the girl's eyes and Amanda couldn't quite figure out what it was.

"What I mean is…. When someone as precious as you comes around with no one missing them… then all your pretty things could be mine…"

It was the most insidious thing Amanda had ever heard but she couldn't move. Sitting frozen stiff in shock she prayed that she heard the girl wrong. She was so pleasant and friendly the night before wasn't she? But then her dad's jokes and his twisted sense of humour…maybe he wasn't even her father…

"I think I better leave now," said Amanda and she stood up urgently to leave.

"You're not going anywhere!" Lucy also stood up and was several inches taller than the governess.

Amanda was startled at the girl's aggression but how much could Lucy hurt her? She looked about the table and saw a large bread knife in the center. Lucy could hurt her a great deal. And the girl noticed Amanda's terrified glances too.

"Oh you like the look of this?" Lucy picked up the knife and tossed it about in her hand playfully before lunging forward, feigning a fencing attack. She laughed maniacally as she looked at the fear in Amanda's eyes. Her heart raced in joyous harmony as the girl before her feared for her life. "Oh you don't like it? Scared are we?" she tilted her head to the side like a little child and pouted. "Aaaw but I just want to help you fix your problems… I just want to help you… DIE!" Lucy's entire demeanour and face changed so rapidly that she was no longer the good Samaritan that Amanda was hoping she would be. It was clear that she wasn't joking anymore.

"You're a monster!" Amanda moved away from the table and flung a chair in front of her to create a makeshift barrier between herself and the girl. "Just stay away from me!" her screams were frantic.

However, a noise momentarily distracted the girls and they both looked away as the doorknob of the front door rattle. In stepped the diamond jawed gent Vincent and he looked pleased at the hectic spectacle that stood before him.

"Oh good! You two have become well acquainted,"

"She's trying to kill me!" Amanda screamed.

"Well of course she is darling," the man spoke rather sarcastically with a hint of flamboyance. "Why else did you think we picked you up and brought you here? To help you?" and he laughed so loudly that it made Amanda jump.

"You're both just awful!" she glanced about in a panic looking for some sort of weapon but there was none.

Her breaths now came rapidly and her concentration was so focussed that she was certain she could hear the blood rushing in her ears. She had to get out of here immediately. She had to get home.

~

"Well sheriff she'll be ok," the doctor was standing over Helen with a stethoscope in his hand and a stern expression on his face. "She's somewhat fragile and her blood pressure's a little low but she'll be ok. Some children are just more sensitive to stress than others," he reassured Terrence.

They were in Helen's bedroom where he had placed her after she fainted. He was in such a state of worry that he was convinced that if he were to leave her alone even for a moment that she could die. But he managed to see reason and left her alone only for a few minutes so he could get the attention of the doctor. He looked down to the old man now and wondered when the old boy was going to retire. The older he got the more he looked as though he hated his job and his patients. In fact he was Terrence's doctor when he was a boy and he was a somewhat grumpy and temperamental old soul then.

"Yeah she'll be up and playing about in no time," the old man stood up.

"Thanks so much for seeing her," Terrence shook his hand gratefully.

"Hmmmm…. As always," the old man put his glasses back on and squinted through them as he looked upwards to the sheriff who towered nearly a foot above him. "Tell me Mr Evans… is there anything about Helen that I should know about?"

"What are you getting at?"

"I just mean that… Is she under any undue stress at all?"

Terrence knew what the old man was talking about. "No… nothing out of the ordinary,"

"I see… and her governess? Is she around to care for her today?"

"No… she is not,"

"I see… Well good day sheriff," and he shook the man's hand again before walking downstairs. "I'll let myself out," he called back to Terrence.

"What a snide bastard," he muttered to himself. Terrence was sure he just came out here to pry and get some gossip. No doubt the entire town would know in the next few minutes that Amanda was gone and Helen had lost her mind with the stress of missing her.

It wasn't even midday yet and the day had got off to a bad start. Terrence felt the urge to head downstairs and pour himself a brandy but he stopped himself. Just the thought of Helen being upset made him want to fix everything and make sure she never worried about another thing ever again. She now lay in her pink sheets with a little more color flushing into her cheeks.

"She's coming back isn't she?"

"I don't know sweety…. I mean yes! Well… I mean I hope so,"

"But I want Mom to come home now!"

Terrence was shocked at what he heard and he felt a lump in his throat that was impossible to swallow. Of course Amanda was Helen's Mom… and she was going to be a great mother to his next child.

~

"Please! Just let me go! I won't tell anybody. I promise," Amanda was trying to negotiate with her captures but they weren't falling for her desperate pleas.

They both laughed in her face. Lucy's face was the most distorted of all, with the pleasure of terror etched into her eyes. The front door was still wide open though. If Amanda could just distract them for a second she could get through and run out to ride the nearest horse away and back to Wattsville. They could see her intentions though and so crowded around her even more, making a very distinct barrier between Amanda and the door.

"You stupid girls are always getting yourselves into trouble… always running away and expecting people to save you. Well guess what? You're not worth saving. Nobody wants you. that's why you're out here all alone. I could kill you where you stand and no one would even notice. You're nothing…" the man pulled a gun out from his belt and pointed it towards Amanda's head.

Lucy meanwhile grew excited at the prospect of seeing bloodshed and started to grin like a lunatic.

"Do it Daddy! Do it!" she laughed and jumped up and down on the spot like a crazy child.

"You're wrong!" shouted Amanda. "People will miss me! I have a family,"

They both laughed at her again.

"I do… I have a family. I live with Sheriff Evans over at Wattsville. He'll be out looking for me right now… or his men will be,"

Lucy and her father looked nervous for a moment but then began their verbal attack again:

"You're lying… a sheriff's wife wouldn't be lost out in the wilderness,"

"Yeah you're lying! You're just some hussy! A slut! A girl who always wants to get her own way just because she's young and pretty, you're all the same" Lucy spat her vitriolic words at Amanda. "You harlots are always causin' trouble out here…"

"I'm not lying," Amanda changed tact and decided to talk calmly and confidently. "You can ask anyone… I'm with the sheriff.

"No you're not," said the man.

"Yes she is…" a mysterious voice came from behind the barrel of a loaded shotgun that lingered in the open doorway.

Lucy and her father spun round surprised.

"Who the hell are you?" Lucy considered jumping forward and stabbing the intruder but that was until she caught sight of his uniform.

She immediately dropped the knife and flung her hands up in surrender. Her father looked appalled at her giving up so easily but even he had to admit to himself that they were in a sticky situation. He relented eventually and begrudgingly placed his gun down on the table with a great reluctance.

"I'm sure we can talk this out… can't we deputy?"

"I'm afraid not," said Tony who then entered the house with his gun still held high.

Amanda's eyes lit up when she saw her old friend. A great relief swept over her and she ran to his side as he outstretched an arm.

"Someone's gonna be very happy to see you when you get home," he led her outside.

CHAPTER 22

"It's not true…" Amanda said with worry in her voice. "He won't be pleased to see me,"

Tony was walking her up the track to the house and although she was more excited than ever to see Terrence and Helen she couldn't help but feel wary.

"He was the one that told me to leave in the first place,"

"Listen kid… Men do stupid things when they're in love. They'll fall into the arms of the wrong woman and push away the most important ones in their life… just so they don't have to admit to themselves that they're in love."

Amanda looked perplexed. "I don't think I can ever know what goes on in Terrence's head,"

"I don't think you even have to know. All you need to realize is that he made a terrible mistake last night. He told me so. He wanted you back more than you could even imagine,"

"Hmmmm….."

"You don't sound convinced,"

"I'm not," Amanda said tersely as they reached the house.

"Well you can believe me or not… I don't care. But you'll soon see when you get in that house… He'll be all over you like a puppy." He laughed as he knocked loudly on the door.

"Who's there?" Terrence's voice came angrily from inside.

"Why it's your very own deputy and I have a surprise or ya!"

Terrence ran to the door and flung it open to see Amanda standing in front of him. His eyes were dark and exhausted as his sleepless, stressed body was brought to life at the sight of her.

"Amanda! Thank God!" he wrapped his arms around her tightly and kissed her face over and over. "Thank God….Thank God," He repeated like a mantra. "I'm so sorry…. Please forgive me,"

"You'll be wanting her to forgive you a lot more when you hear about the scrape I just got her out of," Tony interrupted.

Terrence looked up and his gratefulness turned to concern.

"A scrape? What happened?" he looked down to the girl and she began to cry. "You're shaking…. You better come inside and tell me everything."

~

Helen was sitting at the kitchen table as if nothing had happened at all. She swung her legs playfully and hummed as she twiddled a strand of hair that between her fingers.

"Quiet sweety," Terrence held onto her hand and turned back to Tony and Amanda. "Are you being serious? They were trying to kill you!"

Amanda nodded solemnly.

"So how did you know where to find her?" he asked Tony sceptically.

"Do you know how much people talk in this god damn town?" he laughed. "I knocked on Mrs Wheen's door first and she said that she had seen Amanda walking down the road with a suitcase. She thought it was strange and immediately told her son. He then went out to work in the field with a friend of and they saw that a gentleman on a white horse was following her. Later that night they were in the tavern in town and happened to mention it to Betty who remembered the white horse from a few weeks earlier. It belonged to a "sharp suited Lothario" she said and one of the other girls from the tavern recognized his description. Apparently he can be somewhat of a high roller and a lady lover at times. Anyway she told Lianne who then told me when I visited her later. I'll be honest in that it took a little while to track down his house but I got there eventually," he smiled feeling like the best god damn policeman on earth.

"That's good old fashioned police work I tell ya," laughed Terrence. "And these sons of bitches are down at the station now?"

Tony nodded but Amanda looked frightened.

"What are you going to do?" she asked.

"Nothing they don't deserve…" Terrence said ominously.

~

The gallows towered over the citizens of Wattsville as the crowd gathered in front of it. It hadn't rained for months but on this morning the skies had opened up and a torrent of water was splashing down. However, not a single person moved to get out of its way but rather there were more people than ever standing beneath the black clouds.

"I heard they killed nearly a hundred girls," a whisper came from in front of Amanda and she noticed that the woman who gossiped underneath a handkerchief had turned around to sneak a glance at her.

The governess was standing at the back of the crowd so that less people would notice her. Terrence squeezed her hand in support but his eyes didn't waver from the gallows. On top of the wooden structure stood two hooded figures with ropes around their necks and any second now they would drop. However Amanda didn't want to see them die, she wanted answers instead.

"Why do people do such bad things?" she gazed up to Terrence but he didn't look down at her.

"Some people are just pure evil," was all he said.

Amanda was sure that she could see the reflection of the storm clouds in his eyes as she searched for a flicker of emotion. But all she saw was Terrence's stern face and clenched jaw. In amongst the crowd in front of her the couple could hear the occasional whisper as people discussed the spectacle before them.

"They picked on runaways,"

"The man was a woman hater,"

"I hear the young girl was behind everything,"

"God freaks!"

"I hear they slaughtered hundreds of people! Roamed the countryside at night and killed anyone who came near!"

"They pretended to be father and daughter… what sick people!"

"All the bodies were found under the kitchen floorboards you know…"

The truth was that the myth behind the two was larger than they were. That's not to say that they weren't terrible people for they were in fact murderers and they were also husband and wife. Somewhere along the line it had come into their consciousness that a great plague of harlots was covering the earth. Being the most Biblical and God fearing folk they genuinely thought they were doing a service to Jesus by ridding the state of these poor girls. Many of them came from violent homes and were running away to something better. None of them could have guessed that they would be picked up by the most violent of couples known to man. In the space of ten years Lucy and Vincent De Gaulle had murdered around 30 young girls and celebrated each kill with a visit to church.

Betty turned around and saw that Amanda was hiding beneath the roof of the church. She split herself from the crowd and ran through the rain to meet the couple.

"I just wanted to come over and say thank you," she spoke rather enigmatically.

"What on earth could you possibly be thanking me for?" Amanda asked.

"Years ago… I had a family. I thought I had everything but it's amazing how much you can take for granted," she turned her head and a tear escaped the corner of her eye. "I had a daughter once, I also had a husband. He was a beast mind you and was always beating on my girl. One day I woke up to find that my daughter Virginia wasn't there. She had run away into the night to escape her father's fists. I'll always regret that I never stopped him but I thought I was powerless…" her shoulders sagged under the weight of her guilt.

"That's so terrible. I'm so sorry," Amanda stretched out an arm and placed her hand on the woman's shoulder.

"I thought she would come back… I always thought she'd come home to her mama," Betty began to sob. "But she didn't… but thanks to you and that deputy finding those monsters…" she began to stagger her words as she choked on tears. "Thanks to you and Tony I now know where she went," her words trailed off.

"I'm so sorry. I had no idea… Are you sure?"

"I'm sure alright," she reached into her purse and pulled out a necklace. "They found this under the kitchen. I gave it to her on her fifteenth birthday," the sobs rushed through her body again and she placed the necklace back in her purse.

"I really didn't do anything," Amanda felt a little confused.

"If it weren't for you they would have never been caught," said Betty before she nodded a hello at Terrence and walked back into the crowd to watch her daughter's murderers hang.

"That's a warped logic ain't it?" said Amanda to Terrence.

"I guess it's kinda true though… in a funny sort of way. Maybe fate sent you out to that place so that you'd be found… along with the other girls,"

"I never had you as the fate believin' kinda guy," Amanda touched his face.

They both looked up to the gallows and the rain began to pour even heavier.

"Is killing them the right thing to do?" she asked.

"I believe so… yes," Terrence nodded.

The group of men in black set about the final touches and before long the crowd fell completely silent. People gazed on open mouthed at what they were about to see. It wasn't very often that you'd get to see such a thing happen in your town. Eventually the executioner arrived on the gallows like a star actor arriving on stage. People cheered at his entrance and he even took a perverse bow. Amanda looked at the size and shape of the figure but couldn't guess who the executioner could be.

"Why do they always wear masks?" another question for the sheriff.

"I've never been so sure about that," he said as he kept his eyes in front of him.

Amanda thought something looked familiar about the man on stage. Something about the way he walked, his big rounded shoulders and his upbeat demeanour. But Amanda put her thoughts to the back of her mind as he made his way to the two figures of Vincent and Lucy. She felt a twinge in her stomach and thought about the baby inside of her. Could it hear what was going on? Could it feel her fear? She placed her hand to her stomach and tried to feel it somehow. Soon enough it would be kicking.

The crowd cheered as the executioner grabbed hold of the ropes that lead to the noose around Lucy's neck. Amanda wondered why he had chosen her first. Was it so that her husband could suffer knowing that she was dying next to him? The governess felt sick at the thought and looked to the ground as the cheers grew louder. A moment later the sound of the floor of the gallows was heard as it was pulled away. The crowd cheered louder and the sound of the rope creaking against the wood seemed to carry on the wind but still Amanda didn't look up.

CHAPTER 23

A happy month had passed since the drama of Amanda going missing. She might have been away a short while but the impact on the couple couldn't have been any bigger.

"You'll never leave again will you?" Terrence asked her again as they lay side by side in the moonlight.

"You can stop asking me that!" that sunny laugh. "I'm not going anywhere! And besides what am I going to do? Waddle out of here?"

Terrence laughed too. "I think you're so beautiful with your big belly," he smiled and kissed her on the cheek.

"It's going to get a hell of a lot bigger!"

He wasn't sure it could happen but somehow Amanda became even more beautiful during pregnancy. Her face shone with the perfect rosy glow and her body became even more luscious. He loved the feeling of her new figure in his arms and he loved the warmth that came from her. And of course he adored the way it made her breasts grow even larger and more voluptuous. More than ever he couldn't keep his hands off of her and right now in the middle of the night he wanted to tear off her nightgown and take big handfuls of her in his hands.

Amanda could see the lustful look in his eyes and moved closer to him. I'm not made of glass you know, I'm not going to break. You can touch me all you want,"

Terrence didn't need to be told a second time. He rolled on top of her as carefully as he could so that he didn't hurt her bump. He ran his hands over her stomach and kissed her softly. He felt the desperate need to consume her body in its entirety. He wanted to feel every single part of her all at one and he needed to be in side of her.

In the gentlest manner he moved up the bed so that he was kneeling beside her head. As softly as he could he unbutton the top of her night gown and relished the sight of her growing breasts. He lightly brushed his hands over the top of her hard nipples and loved the way they felt in his palm. Leaning over her he sucked and felt her areola in his mouth. He loved the bumpiness of it and the hardness as she got more aroused. She instantly let out a heavy breath and arched her back with a deep sigh. He ran his tongue down the centre of her body all the way down to her stomach as he caressed her softly with his fingertips.

Amanda sat up and grabbed his hands.

"You can be rougher if you want," she had that naughty twinkle in her eyes.

"I can't… Right now you're more precious than ever. Please… let me kiss you all over and worship your body,"

He lay her back down and began to kiss the length of her legs. Occasionally his lips would reach the top of her thighs and he'd feel her quiver in anticipation but then he'd pull away to tease her. A couple times she grabbed hold of his hair and tried to keep him there but he'd pull away regardless. He wanted this to last forever.

His tongue eventually lapped softly at her sex but only very slightly. She writhed beneath his touch and let out a soft moan. He knew this was one of her favorite things and he took an immense pleasure in making her cum. His favorite thing though was to tease her and the longer it took him to make her orgasm the harder she came.

He moved away from her for a moment just so he could look at her body. Lying down beside her he cuddled her close and placed an arm over her stomach.

"Why have you got to tease me like that!" she jokingly berated him.

"I just down want you to have all your fun at once," he whispered slowly into her ear.

The sound of Terrence whispering was the most thrilling and captivating noise Amanda could hear. She couldn't explain it but just like the whooshing sound of the belt the cadences of Terrence's voice drove shivers up her spine and tingles felt like they would burst out of her ears and neck. It was the most comforting and warm sensation and all he had to say was a few words before she fell in love with him all over again.

"I know you like this… a whole lot," Terrence continued whispering. "Do you think you could cum just hearing my voice?"

Amanda didn't doubt for a second that she couldn't. "Uhuh…" she writhed in pleasure as she leant into him, his breath tickling the skin of her neck.

She shivered all over and broke out in delicious goose bumps. All she wanted was to have her hands all over him. Sliding a hand up his shirt she felt the taught and tight muscles that rippled beneath his skin. She especially loved the hardness of his stomach, the contrast between the rock solid harshness of his abs against the softness of the way he loved.

Terrence slid a hand between her legs and felt the slick wetness on his fingers. He guessed that she was close already and so he leaned in close to her cheek and whispered "You're so beautiful when you're turned on you know that?"

She writhed up to meet his hand and moaned loudly.

"There's nothing better than watching you cum," his soft whispers again.

Terrence started to move his hand faster as he brushed his fingertips over her clitoris harder. He began sensing that she was about to climax, the quivers in her thighs getting stronger and her screams getting louder. He pulled his hand away right at the crucial moment and Amanda was infuriated. She jokingly slapped the top of his head and laughed.

"You can be so cruel!"

"I can show you cruel," he smiled.

He positioned himself between her legs, holding her buttock up with his arms. Instantly he clamped his lips around her and sucked on her clit feeling the juice of her in his mouth. She screamed loudly and began to shake again. But he pulled away.

"Aaaaargh! Terrence! Don't stop,"

"You lie back and don't complain,"

"Urgh….." Amanda gripped at the bedsheets hard with frustration.

And he started again. Sucking hard on her clitoris he could feel how hot she was, how swollen she was in his mouth and how close she was to the best orgasm of her life. Once again he pulled away.

Amanda let out the most agonized scream as though she was being tormented.

"How could you?" she screamed at him but he only laughed.

He moved his mouth back to her again but this time he just tickled her ever so gently as he brushed his tongue over her. Just so gently and softly as if he was barely there and she squirmed beneath him, desperate for him to touch her more. But he pulled away again. Terrence could hear her panting above him but he wanted to tease her just for a moment longer. And so he began to blow lightly on her clitoris and even though it was barely a touch Amanda was so close to climax that even that was enough to send her thighs shaking. Eventually Terrence relented and leaned in to suck on her and he pulled at her clitoris hard with his lips. She orgasmed straight away and let out the loudest scream as her legs shook so violently that Terrence thought they were clamped around his head.

Her fingers were still gripping at Terrence's hair when Amanda regained her breath.

"I love you so much," she sighed deeply. "Will you come up here and hold me?"

"Of course, as always,"

He lay beside her and held her close. They kissed for a moment and looked into each other's eyes.

"I think it's about time that I return the favour,"

"Oh really?" Terrence raised her eyebrows.

"Yah….." she slid her hand into the front of his underwear and felt his girth in his hand.

They had made love more times than Amanda could remember but she was still always surprised at the size of him.

"No wonder you got me pregnant so fast," she giggled as she began working her hand up and down the length.

He instantly felt intense pleasure wash over him and he groaned under her touch. But she pulled away and laughed mischievously.

"You devil!" Terrence grabbed hold of her arms to bring her closer.

"I'm just giving what I got," she smiled.

But he wasn't able to control himself as well as she could and so he quickly rolled her on top of him and moved his hands quickly all over her. Amanda felt herself yield at his touch and she slid down slowly onto his penis. She rode the tip first for a few seconds until she got used to his length and then she took it a little further. And then further again and then another few inches until she was smoothly pushing his entire length into her. It felt immeasurably good to Terrence who grunted as he watched her bounce up and down in front of him. Finally he couldn't hold it much longer and he clamped his hands around her hips tightly and drove himself up into her as fast as possible over and over until he shot himself into her in what felt like the biggest release of his life.

Amanda fell back onto her side of the bed panting "That was the best,"

"I think it gets better the more we do it," he gasped.

"I think so too,"

Once they both regained themselves they lay close as Terrence cuddled into her warm body from behind. Amanda felt that she was growing sleepy but just before her eyes closed she spoke softly.

"We'll always be together won't we?"

"Of course! Why would you even need to ask?"

"Just checking," she said.

"Well don't ask again because you won't have to check,"

"I just worry that you'll get bored of me… once the baby is born,"

"That's ridiculous!" he rolled her round so that he could see her face "That's silly thinking kitten, really," and he kissed the end of her nose.

"I hope so,"

"Well if I love you baby bump and all I'm certainly not going to be bored with you after he's born…"

His words hung in the air for a second before Amanda picked up on what he said.

"You really think it'll be a boy?"

"I just kinda thought so yeah," he said rather arrogantly.

"And why's that?" she laughed.

"I dunno… I just think a boy…" although he didn't explain why.

Amanda thought it would be beautiful to have a boy. A little handsome prince to keep the little princess Helen happy and she would make a terrific sister, she could tell. She wondered what he would look like and she imagined him to be as dashingly handsome as his father but with the softness of his mother. No doubt he'd be impossibly tall and square jawed with a head of dark, rustic hair. She would love to see what color eyes he would have and what his voice would sound like. If he was anything like his father he was going to be a real heartbreaker.

"I'm going to start putting things in the nursery," Amanda said sleepily.

"That would be nice," Terrence yawned.

CHAPTER 24

Mrs Wheen had tears in her eyes when she saw Amanda step out in her wedding dress.

"I can't believe the day has arrived so fast,"

"I know! I can't believe it either. I've spent the last few months thinking about nothing else and hoping the day would hurry up and get here and it'll be over in matter of hours!" Amanda started to well up with tears too.

"I think you look like a real princess!" Helen declared as she stepped out next.

This time Mrs Wheen seemed to lose control of herself as she squealed in delight at the sight of the little girl in the frilly pink dress.

"No pumpkin I think the real princess is you!" and she bopped Helen on the nose.

"And have you got your flowers ready?"

Helen nodded.

"Good girl. I think you'll make the most delightful little flower girl, you really will,"

"Thanks Mrs Wheen!"

"What have I told you about saying that? Mrs Wheen was my mother. I'm just Aunty Sylvia to you,"

Helen nodded again and blushed behind a bouquet of flowers.

Meanwhile Amanda was busy looking into a nearby mirror and examining her stomach.

"Oh dear do I look as horribly fat as I feel?"

"Well you're 8 months pregnant so you better," the old lady laughed. "I remember when I was having my first. I'd never felt sicker in my life for the first three months but then as I got bigger I'd never been healthier. I put it down to all that gorgeous milk my husband insisted on giving me. Still felt like a big sow though, just so big and heavy," and she went quiet for a second as she remembered far back into her youth.

"I can't wait to have a baby brother," Helen blurted out. "I'm goin' to dress him up like a cowboy,"

The two women laughed. "You can do that as much as you like," smiled Amanda and she kissed Helen on the forehead.

"Well good Lord we better get you moving!" Mrs Wheen was almost shouting as she noticed the time.

~

The church bell was ringing as Amanda walked slowly up the steps with Helen. Although she felt so tremendously happy there was still a pang of sadness as she entered the church and everyone turned to see her. She had always dreamed that were she to marry that her father would of course walk her up the aisle but here she was with Tony by her side instead. She had a sudden longing to visit her family.

"Thank you," she said quietly as she linked her arm into Tony's. "You're a terrific friend,"

"I love you both a great deal," he smiled as he walked her down the aisle to the sound of the old organ playing.

Most of the town had turned up to see the big day not only because it was the sheriff who was getting married but also because they felt they owed it to Amanda after what she had been through. And as Terrence looked into her eyes as he saw her in her dress for the first time everyone could see how happy she made him, and of course how happy she made the little bouncing Helen who was by their side with an enormous grin on her face. Amanda glanced out quickly to the crowd and saw that not a single person was looking at her stomach. She breathed a sigh of relief and turned back to Terrence as the priest began to speak.

They said their vows with dignity and their eyes never left each other as they promised their futures to one another. There was barely a dry eye in the building either as people watched Terrence be so happy. Many of the people in the church remembered being here for him the first time round and the misery that ensued with Evangeline. Many people made a silent prayer for Amanda and the baby and hoped that she would be safe.

After the ceremony everyone rallied around the happy newlyweds at their home and Helen, though shy and wary of everyone soon relaxed and fell into the swing of the festivities. But it wasn't long until Terrence had to put her to bed.

"You made a terrific flower girl today," he kissed her forehead as she snuggled under the bedsheets with her favorite soft toy, a bunny rabbit named Rupert.

"I think Tony made a good man,"

Terrence smiled "I think so too," and he kissed her again before blowing out the candle and saying goodnight.

Downstairs people were still happy and drinking and congratulating the couple. Betty was the drunkest of them all and when she slapped Terrence on the back he felt as though he had been winded.

"Take it easy lady," he joked as she drank another shot of whiskey.

Tony meanwhile was laughing at her from the other side of the kitchen and he eventually approached his best pal.

"I think she needs taken home,"

"I didn't figure she was your type," said the sheriff sarcastically as he looked down to his glass of milk.

"You know what I mean," Tony rolled his eyes.

"I think she needs a bucket of cold water and a slap," he joked.

"Argh she'll be fine, she's a tough old lady," laughed Tony "She could drink us all under the table,"

"She sure could… But erm… Tony… I wanted to say something,"

The deputy looked up from his glass with a quizzical look on his face.

"It's nothing serious," Terrence continued. "I just wanted to say thank you… for encouraging me to do the right thing. You're a real pal,"

"It's nothing…" Tony looked away feeling slightly embarrassed. "So when do you leave tomorrow?"

"First thing in the morning,"

The couple were to be heading out west for their honeymoon but it would be a short and sweet trip. Not only did Wattsville need their sheriff back but Amanda was worried about the baby.

"Well I'll miss ya buddy," Tony jovially punched his friend in the arm.

"I'll only be gone a week!" Terrence chuckled.

"But I'll have no one around to make fun of!"

And they both laughed as they headed out to the porch.

CHAPTER 25

The three girls were giggling insanely as they sat out on the porch with their plates of cherry pie.

Bertha looked to her little sister and felt enormously proud. "I was so worried about you, so terribly worried and mama and pa too!"

"I'm sorry girls," Amanda sighed. "It's been a strange kinda year,"

"I can tell!" chimed in Scarlett. "You head off to work for a little Christian family and come back with a big handsome sheriff for a husband and two children!"

"I never thought you would be the first of us to have a baby," said Bertha with a hint of bitterness in her voice.

"Me neither!" said Scarlett. "I never would have guessed it,"

"But your little girls are both little angels!"

"Aaw thanks! You know we were so convinced it was going to be a boy that we even painted the nursery blue!" Amanda laughed. "Well we had to change that quickly!"

"He would obviously have been too handsome for the world to handle so God gave you a little girl,"

"Yeah...." Amanda turned around to look into the window. "She's the most gorgeous little thing, a real doll and Helen just loves her so dearly,"

"So tell me…" Bertha leaned in. "What's it like to be a wicked step-mother?"

"Hey! I'm nothing of the sort,"

They all giggled.

"In fact I'm a lovely mother to Helen,"

"And how could you not be? Those eyes!"

And the two sisters also turned around to look in the window at their parents playing with their grandchildren.

Helen had really grown up over the last year and as Amanda looked through the glass at her step-daughter she saw that she looked so much like Evangeline. She wondered how Terrence would cope with that as she got older and looked more and more like his first wife. And she wondered how much he still missed her.

A lot had changed since the couple were married. The house was redecorated and the attic was cleared out. Amanda never did find out what happened to the mysterious trunk but she never wanted to ask but rather set about converting the attic space into a beautiful and spacious play area for the children.

The first month of marriage though was a little tough as Amanda was fit to drop at any moment and Terrence was terrified. He kept running home from the station at any moment to check on her and was always delighted to see that she was still ok. On the day she went into labor the tension in the house was enormous as Terrence paced the floors downstairs nervously over and over as he listened overhead to the sound of Amanda screaming. Eventually he heard the tiny cry of a baby and he'd ran upstairs energetically to burst into his bedroom. He found Amanda cradling a tiny bundle and she had tears in her eyes and sweat on her brow but she'd never looked so beautiful and serene.

"It's a girl!" the doctor interjected Terrence's reverie.

"A girl?"

The doctor and Amanda both nodded.

"That's wonderful!" he said genuinely. "Another special little princess, how marvellous," and he felt as though he was close to tears with happiness.

"Have you thought of a name?" asked the doctor who, grumpy as ever, was packing up his things already as he was eager to leave.

"A name? Well… it was going to be Tony,"

"How about Antonia?" Amanda suggested through her haze of post pregnancy euphoria.

"That's brilliant! Antonia it is!" and he bent down to look at his daughter's face. He kissed her so very gently and smiled at Amanda. "She's perfect. Just like you," and he gave her a hug.

"She has your eyes," she whispered dreamily.

"Can I see her now?" a little voice came from the other side of the door and Helen barged in eagerly. "I want to see her!"

"Have you been listening in on us this whole time?" Terrence laughed as he scooped her up to carry her over to the bed.

"Of course I have!" she said cheekily. "I wanted to make sure Amanda would be ok,"

"You're a very sweet girl," said Amanda as she placed an arm around her husband and step-daughter.

As the doctor finished packing his things and left the family behind Amanda was left in her bed with all three of the most precious people in the world surrounding her and she finally felt as though she weas a complete person with everything she'd ever wanted.

Now as she sat out on the porch with her sisters that feeling hadn't left her and she watched her little angels through the window with a warmth deep in her heart.

"I'm so jealous of you!" Scarlett was swooning at her sister's life.

"Me too!" Bertha agreed. "The way he looks at you! Urgh….."

Terrence was sitting next to his father in law but hadn't taken his eyes off his wife. Her pale eyes and tumbling dark curls were as beautiful as ever to him and he couldn't wait to see how she'd grow up over the next few years. He had no doubt that she would only get even more beautiful the older she got.

"I bet he's a real stallion in bed!" laughed Bertha. She was joking but she genuinely wanted to know the juicy details.

"Bertha!" Scarlett flung a cherry pip at her big sister. "You're disgusting you know that! That's her husband!"

"Hey, I can dream can't I?" Bertha laughed again.

"Ladies please…" Amanda interrupted their childish shenanigans. "If you must know he fucks like a jack hammer and is the size of a Trojan," she smirked.

Her two sisters erupted into a fit of squealing and Bertha was blushing like never before. The front door opened and the girls' mother stood before them looking as glowing as a newlywed herself. The sudden appearance of her youngest daughter and the sight of having grandchildren was the best most glorious thing she had ever wished for and she was revelling in the duties of being a grandmother.

"Girls!" she spoke like an old matron. "Care to come inside for second helpings of pie?"

And the three sisters headed into the house as though they had never been apart.

The End

Read on for a free book sent straight to your inbox. ☺

FREE FOR YOU! *Spanked: Mail Order Bride Western Romance*

Receive a FREE copy of Spanked when you sign up for Lolita London's mailing list!

The hottest Mail Order Bride Western Romance!

Click here and have the book in your inbox in seconds

He's a wealthy southern gentleman that any women would go through hell and high water to marry. So why has he secured a bride through a mail order bride service?

Madeline doesn't know, and she's concerned by rumors of his dominant personality - but rumors are just rumors after all, and she knows he's one of the few eligible bachelors left.

A letter in the mail, a hurried goodbye, and a long train ride later she meets her new husband - Robert Cortege. Tall and handsome, she begins to think that everything will work out after all.

Little does Madeline know her life is about to spiral out of her control, and there's only one man who will have the power to put her life back together - Mr. Cortege. That is, if he doesn't push her to the breaking point first.

There will be no mistake as to what is expected of her - total submission. She'll spend a lot of time bent over his knee with a bare bottom, and torn between pleasure and pain as the charming millionaire wastes no opportunity to make her moan shamelessly, no matter who's in earshot.

With a sick mother in another city, and multiple harlots chasing her husband and threatening to end her marriage soon after it begins, she doesn't know whether to fight tooth and nail or hope everything works out.

After all, if there's one thing Mr. Cortege teaches her, it's just how good surrender can feel.

This is a full length, stand-alone novella with a satisfying ending. No cliffhangers.

This historical western romance involves adult themes of spanking, sexual submission, alpha male domination, first time lovemaking, and domestic discipline.